FICTION

INQUIRIES & ADVERTISING

Address: Suite 22, 509 Commissioners Road West, London, Ontario, N6J 1Y5
Advertising: Email info@mysterymagazine.ca
Editor: Kerry Carter **Publisher:** Chuck Carter **Cover Artist:** Robin Grenville Evans
Submissions: https://mysterymagazine.ca/submit.asp

BACK DOWN TO BLACK

Andrew Welsh-Huggins

They met in a coffee shop off Grand Avenue, the smell of roasting beans filling the air. Espresso machine hissing in the background. Bottles of flavored syrups, red and purple and green, lining the back wall like something you'd put on the mantel at Christmas. All the same to Carter, who was pretty much a Folger's guy when and if he drank the stuff, but it's not like they were there for the beverages. And truth be told, it was nice to be out in public again. Four of them at the table. Langford, who was running the show. A big guy, Fritz, who didn't say a lot. And Dr. Zhang, waiting expectantly but not over anxiously for the meeting to proceed.

"Any problems?" Langford said.

"None," Carter said, patting the upper right pocket of his tan utility vest.

"And nobody ..."

"Nobody," Carter said. "Why you're paying me."

"Great. In that case, I think we're all set?" Langford nodded at Fritz. An envelope just over half the size of a burnt clay brick appeared atop the table. They were seated at the back of the coffee shop, just in case, but this time of day, early morning rush past, the crowd inside was thin and nobody was around to notice.

"Fujian Province?" Carter said to Dr. Zhang, ignoring the envelope.

"That's right," she said, a look of mild surprise on her face. "You've done your research. Most people think I'm from Hubei, because of my work in Wuhan the last time."

"I like seafood," Carter said. "Fujian cuisine is spicy, but not overwhelming. Sea cucumber is one of my favorites. It's a specialty in Xiamen, of course. You must miss it."

"It's true," Dr. Zhang said. "As much as I like Iowa, it's nearly impossible to get here."

"A good thing."

"Good?" Dr. Zhang said, puzzled.

"Good, because aren't you deathly allergic to seafood? Or should I say, isn't Dr. Ying Zhang? I don't know about you."

The woman froze, staring at Carter for two long seconds before glancing at Langford.

"What are you talking about?" Langford said in a low voice.

"I'm talking about the seafood allergy of Dr. Ying Zhang of Drake University. Which means the person sitting across from me is someone else, which I could have told you anyway because of the difference in their photographs. The situation is a little insulting, to be honest, because it implies you thought I couldn't distinguish between them because they're Chinese and they all look alike to Westerners."

The table was still. The envelope disappeared, replaced by Fritz's hands, each the size of a small catcher's mitt, placed palms down on the table top.

"What do you want?" Langford said.

"I want to wrap up this delivery and get going, is what I want. I'm due in Rapid City tomorrow and my schedule is tight. Even tighter now, apparently."

"I have your money. You have the information. We're both saving lives. What difference does it make at this point?"

"The difference is that the invoice is clear. Delivery directly to Dr. Ying Zhang. No one else."

"We could just take it from you," Langford said quietly. He looked at Fritz and then back at Carter, and the implication was clear. Fritz, who towered over Carter to begin with, might not have been twice Carter's weight, but close enough. Not to mention his hands, one of which Carter was pretty sure could cover both of his and leave room for another body part or two.

"Maybe," Carter said. He picked up his spoon and slowly stirred his coffee. "Or maybe I could take this spoon and gouge your eyes out lickety-split and just walk away. Because I really need to get to Rapid."

Ta-ting, ta-ting, ta-ting, went the spoon as he stirred, scraping it in repetitive circles against the porcelain mug's interior.

"In your dreams," Langford said.

Carter removed the spoon and set it on his napkin, watching the coffee stain bloom outward like a small, brown aneurysm. "You're probably right," he said. "But just so we're clear, I don't actually have it on my person." He unbuttoned the utility vest pocket, pulled out an eraser the approximate size and shape of a flash drive, and set it in the middle of the table.

"Where is it?"

"Someplace safe."

Langford and Fritz locked glances.

"Before you get any bright ideas, this is not a scenario where knowing the location will help you," Carter said. "You can pound my toes with a hammer and jam needles into my fingernails and attach car battery cables to my reproductive organs, and don't worry, I'll give it up in about two seconds flat. But the thing is, it has to be me who retrieves it. In person, photo ID, verified signature, the whole nine yards. All the pain in the world is not going to help you there."

"So, we're at an impasse."

"Just the opposite, in fact."

"Meaning?"

"We just need to try again. Set up another meeting. Simple as pie." Carter glanced at the imposter across the table. "This time with Dr. Zhang—the real doctor. I don't care about your relationship with her, and I don't care what happens to her afterward. But my instructions are clear: the delivery goes to her, and her alone."

"We set that up, you hand it over?"

"To Dr. Zhang. As articulated in the contract."

"How can we be sure?"

"I'm sorry?"

"How can we be sure you'll hand it over?"

Carter picked up his spoon and stirred his coffee again. Ta-ting, ta-ting, ta-ting.

"You can be sure because I've never missed a delivery. That's how."

Carter left them in the coffee shop and walked east on Grand to his Suburban. He walked quickly since it was threatening rain. He got himself inside, buckled up, and pulled away from the curb a minute later. The third guy, not quite as big as Fritz but close, picked him up near Sixth Street in an older model Toyota. He was better than Carter expected and stayed with him until Carter enlisted a couple of Amazon Prime trucks to box him out on East 235 right before the Guthrie Avenue exit. He took surface streets from there to his motel on the North Side, keeping an eye on the sky as he drove.

Carter didn't pretend to understand what all the fuss was about. Another public health emergency looming, you'd have thought everyone would be on the same page. But apparently the information he was being paid to deliver to Dr. Zhang was valuable in ways he hadn't anticipated. There being a market for such information at a time like this was naturally distasteful to Carter. But not so distasteful that he let it distract himself from the job at hand. Delivery directly to the doctor herself. Not imposters in coffee shops accompanied by muscled guys carrying bricks of cash around. Talk about unseemly.

Inside his motel room, Carter lifted the left corner of the mattress and retrieved the plastic soap dish containing the flash drive and put it for real in his pocket. He wondered how they would play it. He wasn't optimistic and he wasn't proven wrong. The text came less than thirty minutes later. The new meet was a parking lot on the far side of Gray's Lake. Arranged that quickly, it meant the real Dr. Zhang was either dead, or would be soon, and they wanted him to join her in that condition by meeting him that far out of the way. No matter what, this delivery was becoming more complicated by the second. And Carter had never cared for complications.

He parked on the side of the lake closest to downtown, on the opposite side from the meet. The sky was dark and the air hung heavy and humid and smelled faintly of diesel fumes that only a gully washer could purge if and when it came. He adjusted the Iowa Cubs ball cap he'd purchased online a week earlier, slipped on a pair of reflective sunglasses, tightened his running belt, patted the belt's pouch, and set off at a slow jog down the trail.

It took him about ten minutes to reach the parking lot on the west side of the vaguely figure-eight lake. He made the van immediately, parked at the far end, near a thick copse of trees close to the river. Two spaces down, the Toyota from earlier in the day. Unoccupied, which meant they were putting all their resources into a single force inside the van. He wondered if he'd last even two seconds with needles in his fingernails. He doubted it. He kept running until he was past the parking lot. He stopped by a cottonwood starting to shed its fuzz, pulled his phone from his pouch and texted Langford. *See you in 10 minutes.*

OK came the reply.

One minute later Carter ducked into the trees and quietly approached the rear of the van. Thirty yards off, hidden in the woods, he paused and peered through the back window and counted three heads: Langford, Fritz, and the third guy, the one who'd tailed him. No one else, which did not bode well for Dr. Zhang, or the imposter either, come to think of it. Not to mention arriving in Rapid anywhere close to on time. He took a step back, into the trees, and tried to decide whether it was better to call their bluff now or wait until he returned to his motel room. He took another step back and heard a twig snap underfoot and felt cold metal against the back of his neck.

"Nice and easy, ace," a dry voice said. "Don't do anything stupid."

A fourth guy. Of course. He should have guessed, based on the contents of the flash drive and the distasteful market he was learning so much about. Well played, he thought, glancing at the Toyota. The perfect decoy. They must have made him as he jogged past even as he made them. He had to hand it to Langford. He wondered if they had the torture devices in the van or hidden away someplace a little less public.

"Sure," Carter said, and did something stupid, driving his left elbow back into the man's chest. Carter was hardly big enough to do any kind of damage with such a move, which almost any schoolboy could manage better, but it startled No. 4 and the gun barrel slipped off Carter's neck momentarily and he turned and broke the man's nose with his left palm, rocketing his hand forward like a power to the people salute gone terribly wrong. As No. 4 staggered back, blood blooming from both nostrils, Carter reached out and took his gun from him and swung it hard against the left side of his head and opened up a long, red, raw flap of skin. The man screamed and Carter kneed him between his legs and he staggered and Carter did it again and the man went down with a heavy thump like something rolled off the back of a truck. Carter caught his breath and ejected the magazine from the gun and unchambered the live round and tossed those to his left and the gun to his right. He knelt beside the moaning, bloodied man and retrieved the spoon from his running pouch, the one from the coffee shop, and held it firmly in his hand, trying to decide which eye was best. He didn't have much time. Right, he decided at last, and lowered his hand and looked for the correct angle and found it. In a single, smooth, swift motion he gently placed the spoon concave side up on the man's cheek, just a few millimeters below his right eye. He retrieved his phone and snapped a picture and took the spoon back and stood up. He stepped over No. 4 and walked through the woods back to the trail by the river and headed for his Suburban. He had to brush the sweat from his eyes several times as he ran, it was so humid and hot.

Back in the car, Carter texted the picture of No. 4 with the spoon resting on his cheek to Langford.

You have one minute to prove Dr. Zhang is alive.

I need more time came the reply.

50 seconds

Ten seconds passed. Twenty. Carter thought of the trip to Rapid and tried to remember whether the parks on the city's far outskirts were Custer National Forest and Black Hills State Park, or vice versa. He always got it wrong. Vice versa, he thought. No chance he'd have time for a swing through either at this point. A shame, since it was always enjoyable to see bison in the wild. Ten more seconds passed, and his phone vibrated with an in-coming call.

"Carter?"

A man's voice.

"What."

Silence on the line, then a woman's voice, weak-sounding but not defeated.

"This is Dr. Zhang. Who am I speaking with, please?"

Calling from someplace that wasn't the van. Call initiated by a man not in the van.

Which meant a fifth guy.

"Hello?" Dr. Zhang said.

"It's Mercury Carter. Who is Konah Washington?"

"I beg your pardon?"

He repeated the question.

After a pause, she said, "He's a farmer."

"How do you know him?"

"I buy his eggplants at the farmers' market. They're the best in Des Moines."

"He's from Sierra Leone, correct?"

"No," she said firmly. "He's Liberian."

"Thank you," he said, and disconnected. A second later he texted Langford.

Set the meet. Last chance.

The real Dr. Zhang was alive, which was good. Five guys—well, four and a casualty—was not so good. Especially not so good for Dr. Zhang, no matter that she'd be personally receiving the information he was delivering, as required. Which was always a mandate of the job, no matter what the package. Some people just couldn't get that part into their heads, no matter how many times he explained it. The shit they tried to pull. Like scheduling a medical procedure and then arriving with your uncle and expecting the surgeon to operate on him instead. As if. Ten minutes later his phone buzzed.

State capitol steps. Just Zhang and me. Can't get more public.

Carter couldn't dispute it. Putting aside all the aides and visitors and state police coming and going, he was guessing the Statehouse grounds were lousy with security cameras. A place that argued against monkey business. It was a good call. He checked his watch. Pushing two. This way, he could still make Rapid by midnight. Too late for his delivery, but if he knocked it out early enough the next day, he could be back on the road for Ohio at a reasonable hour and home again the following day, assuming he didn't try to just gut it out. At his age he was finding those kinds of drives harder and harder. Yes, it might all work out. Except for the bison. And except that there was a problem with the new plan. A mostly insurmountable one, he realized. He texted his answer.

I'll come to where you've got Zhang. Send the address.

Langford's response took nearly three minutes. Carter knew that interval; time enough to make surprisingly complete arrangements, even within the confines of a mere 180 seconds. The GPS pin dropped with a ping and two words:

Three o'clock.

Google maps showed the address as a generic four-story office building in West Des Moines, 1970s era, banks of dark windows set within a tic tac toe pattern of poured concrete. One of four nestled inside a cloverleaf of winding asphalt drives three minutes off the highway. The kind of offices where big firms relocate after downsizing and start-ups spend as few months as possible before inhabiting old downtown warehouse space with easy brewpub access. Nothing much in-between, business-wise.

Fifteen minutes after leaving his motel, Carter pulled into a gas station around the corner from the building. A grumble of thunder in the distance. Inside, he bought two medium coffees and two medium teas and accepted the clerk's offer of a cardboard carrier for the cups. He was glad he did because the cups were hot to the touch even through the cardboard sleeves that he slipped each one into.

A minute later, he saw what he'd missed on Google. *BUILDING FOR LEASE*, said the large yellow sign outside the entrance, along with an 800-number and an email. Sign facing an empty parking lot, which abutted a run-off retention pond. The 'for lease' sign meaning Langford and company were either squatting or had made temporary, don't ask-don't tell arrangements that spoke to their high level of interest in concealing themselves.

Four guys, though he wasn't sure he could rule out the man with the gun at Gray's Lake, despite the hurt he'd delivered. If not, five was a lot. A lot for a flash drive the size of an eraser. Except for Langford pointing out the obvious. *We're both saving lives.* Just to be safe, Carter retrieved his gun from the glove compartment and tucked it into the holster sewed inside the left flap of his utility vest. Sig Sauer P229, not that he was wedded to it, but standard U.S. Postal Inspection issue, and old habits die hard.

After the deal out by the lake, Carter was counting on two in the lobby to escort him upstairs to the fifth-floor office delineated by the GPS pin. Certainly, the arrangements he would have made. After locking up, he walked toward the entrance, a cup of coffee in each hand, watching his reflection in the glass doors as he approached. He used his right elbow to push the square handicapped door access switch and waited patiently for the doors to swing open. The third guy, the tail, was standing by the elevator, staring at him. He'd made no effort to disguise the cannon strapped to his hip. Beside him, Fritz. Outside, the patter of drops on asphalt as the rain arrived at last.

"Hey—sorry I'm late," Carter said, raising the cups in a gesture of greeting, but slowly so as not to spill any. "Beat the rain at least."

The man with the gun didn't say anything, but instead pressed the button for the fifth floor. Fritz dead-eyed Carter like none of it would matter in another minute or two, which was probably true.

"Hope you guys like coffee," Carter said. "I made both black, just so you know. I never want to presume people take cream or sugar in case they actually don't. Way I figure, you can always go *up* to that if you want, because there's almost always a supply around, you know? Nine out of ten offices, they have a kitchen or a break room or somebody's drawer with all the condiments, even if it's just Sweet'N Low and that powdered creamer stuff. Right? But you can't go back *down* to black. Once you've put that stuff in, you're committed, and if it's not your thing, then you've ruined a perfectly good cup of joe. Anyway, hope it's OK."

Behind them, the elevator door opened with a pleasant ding.

"So, what do you think?" Carter said. "Black OK?"

"I don't drink coffee," the man with the cannon said. Fritz said nothing at all.

"Probably for the best," Carter said, and threw the steaming contents of the cups into each man's face.

Most people, you toss sixteen fluid ounces of liquid heated to an average temperature of 180 degrees Fahrenheit between their eyes, they howl first, then reflexively raise their hands in a nearly simultaneous attempt to assuage the pain that emanates from a scalding burn that's probably going to blister. At least that was Carter's experience. And in fact, that's what Fritz did, stumbling backward and into the open elevator car with a high-pitched yelp as his fingers clawed his face. But training matters, and the guy with the cannon had had it, which was evident because even as he yelled, he reached not for his face but fumbled for the gun on his hip. Carter was impressed, but not enough to stick around to see what happened next.

He made the corner before the shot went off behind him. He stopped just long enough to pull the fire alarm by the entrance to the stairs and was through the door a second later. He was up the first set of stairs in two seconds, rounded the landing, and made the second flight in another two seconds. Second floor. He didn't bother to listen for the sound of pursuit. What difference would it have made? Not to mention being nearly impossible to hear over the teeth-chattering clang of the fire alarm splintering the silence of the empty office building. Stairs, two seconds, landing. Stairs, two seconds. Third floor. Stairs, two seconds, landing. Stairs, two seconds. Fourth floor. Carter was breathing hard now, which he knew was natural because even the fittest athletes struggled with the challenge posed by vertical ascents by stair. Something about the demands of using fast-twitch muscles when your body insisted on the slow-twitch approach. Natural but still kind of bothersome, especially at a time like this. Stairs, two seconds, landing. Stairs 2½ seconds. Fifth floor.

The key word was stairs. As in *stairs*. As in a single word that could be texted to Langford by either Fritz or the guy with the cannon, texted or relayed by phone. Meaning: *he took the stairs up!* Correct that: not by Fritz. Carter saw the way Fritz's fingers raked his eyes when the coffee hit home. It would be the guy with the cannon on his hip, the one who had the training. So: counting the dash around the corner, the pause to pull the fire alarm, the half-second to yank open the door and then the sprint upward, it had taken Carter approximately thirty seconds to elevate his one-hundred-and-fifty-one-pound frame five stories up from the lobby to the door that opened onto the top floor. Back in the lobby, at least a third of that time would be eaten up by the man fumbling for his gun and then getting off a single, errant shot. Then, he would have had to holster the gun or at the very least awkwardly switch hands while he retrieved his phone from a pocket. Next, another second or two to unlock the phone, and then another few seconds to message Langford, text or call, about the situation. *Stairs.* "*Stairs!*" Either way, Carter didn't think any of that could have happened inside of the twenty remaining seconds after the shot. He pushed the door open and burst into the hall.

He'd calculated it correctly, for the most part. No Langford waiting for him, crouched in combat stance as the strobes of the emergency alarm system illuminated him in repeating flashes of white light. No sign of the guy from Gray's Lake, the one who took him from behind with the gun to his neck, which made sense given the way Carter left him. No indication of the fifth guy, the man who'd facilitated the brief call with Dr. Zhang after the incident at the lake. And no Fritz and the guy with the cannon on his hip. So: all as predicted, except for one wrench. He hadn't counted on the sight of the imposter stumbling down the hall toward him, the fake Dr. Zhang, fear and confusion contorting her features as she zigzagged her way toward the bank of elevators, passing a moment later directly in front of him.

"I'll shoot her, Carter. I swear."

"Make it fast if you're going to," Carter answered. "By my count, you have sixty seconds until the first fire truck arrives." Nearly shouting to make himself heard over the alarm, and the sheets of rain lashing the windows, and the whimpering of the imposter as she struggled to free herself from his grip. She quieted as he dug the barrel of the Sig Sauer a little harder into her kidneys. Carter said: "All geared up, it'll take them a while to get up here. Couple minutes. They'll have to go floor by floor. They'll be thorough. But it won't be that long."

"That's what you want? For me to kill her?"

"I want to make my delivery and leave. That's all."

Standing in the small foyer just inside Suite 555. Langford and Zhang not visible, but by the sound of Langford's voice, around the corner by thirty-five, maybe forty feet tops. Carter pictured Langford with his gun to the epidemiologist's head. She was probably bound at her hands and feet, and likely gagged. Langford struck Carter as an overkill kind of guy when it came right down to it.

Langford said, "Last chance."

"Thirty seconds to the truck. Maybe closer to twenty-five."

An interruption behind him. The guy with the cannon burst into the suite, gun in his hand, face an overbaked personal pan pizza of red blotches. He stopped, blinking his rheumy eyes to stare at Carter who stared back at him, then dropped his eyes to indicate the Sig Sauer jammed into the back of a dark-haired woman who—truth be told—looked remarkably like Dr. Ying Zhang.

"Twenty seconds—"

The gunshot loud in the enclosed space. The imposter gave a shriek, gasped, and slumped in Carter's arms. Even the guy with the splotchy face jumped.

Carter didn't let go. He didn't move. He didn't rush around the corner in hopes of capping Langford in the head and trying to rescue Dr. Zhang as she bled out. He stayed put as the imposter trembled in his arms and the man with the gun, making a series of deep, rhythmic, raspy sounds, tried to control his breathing after his ascent up the stairs. Carter waited. He didn't have long. Even over the alarm and the rain, the whoops of the fire trucks' dying sirens were audible from outside as the vehicles pulled up beside the building. An impressive response time, Carter thought. The infrastructure of West Des Moines was in good hands.

"Time's up," Carter shouted, pushing the imposter into the arms of the man with the cannon in his hand. The man gasped, still struggling to find his air. The imposter gave another shriek. Langford appeared a moment later, gun by his side, another guy behind him. The fifth man. Both of them eyeing Carter's Sig Sauer, which was no longer by Carter's side.

"Hope you're happy," Langford said.

"No butter," Carter shouted.

"What?"

"Don't use butter on the burns." He nodded at the man gasping behind him, the imposter clutching him like a child clinging to an oak in a windstorm. "Old wives' tale. Actually makes it worse."

"You have no idea how big a mistake you've made."

Carter used his free hand to reach into his lower left vest pocket. He retrieved the coffee shop spoon, took aim, and flipped it at Langford, dinging him square on the nose.

"I'll be the judge of that," Carter said.

He found Dr. Zhang about how he'd pictured her, confined to a chair two thirds of the way back in the office, tucked into the space between two cubicles, except that her hands were zip tied behind her back and then additionally zip tied to the back of the chair. Overkill, like he thought. He pulled a Swiss army knife from the bottom right pocket of his vest, opened the smaller of two blades, and cut the ties. Dr. Zhang studied him as he worked. When she was freed, he helped her up, made sure she had her balance, and walked her out of the office and into the lobby. He pushed the elevator button for the first floor. They were inside and the door was closing just as he heard the sound of impressively quick responding, all-geared-up firefighters coming through the stairway door. Thorough, like he said.

In the lobby, they passed two more firefighters tending to Fritz, whose face looked like he'd had a swarm of bees for breakfast and a hive of wasps for lunch. A minute after that they were in his Suburban, watching Langford's van speed out of the complex, just avoiding a second, in-coming pumper. Buckled into the passenger seat, Dr. Zhang rubbed her wrists, encouraging the circulation. Carter lifted the two teas from the cardboard carrier and handed her one. She raised the cup to her lips, took a sip, and looked at Carter.

"He said he was going to shoot me."

"He did."

"He gave you an ultimatum, but you called his bluff. With my life on the line."

Carter didn't reply, instead recalling the hole in the cubicle across from Dr.

Zhang that was left by the shot Langford fired in an attempt to draw Carter inside.

"He told me about the seafood allergy. The trap you set at the coffee shop. Very clever."

"I wouldn't exactly say trap."

"What then? Since as I'm guessing you know, I love seafood. And I'm not at all allergic."

"It was a foray. The truth didn't matter—it was her reaction to the thought they might have overlooked something that mattered. That told me all I needed to know."

"A fishing expedition?"

"Good one," Carter said.

"You also agreed to meet him at Gray's Lake, but then reneged and snuck up from behind."

"Something like that."

"Most troubling, you told him you didn't care what happened to me after you made the delivery. He was very specific about that—thought it was rather amusing."

"I may have said something like that."

"May have?"

Carter started the Suburban and turned the heater onto high to clear the window, fogged inside from all the humidity. Rain coming down even harder now. Too hard for anyone to pay them much mind at the moment.

Dr. Zhang said, "How did you know about Konah Washington and the eggplants?"

"I did some research."

"Including the fact I'd know he was from Liberia and not Sierra Leone?"

"That was a lucky guess," he admitted.

"Let me get this straight. You lied, cheated, and then gambled with my life. Is that about right?"

Carter told her that it was.

"Why?"

"The invoice was clear," he said. "Delivery to be made directly to you. No one else. Which reminds me." He reached into the upper pocket of his utility vest, retrieved the flash drive, and handed it to her. In return, she reached into her purse and retrieved an envelope much, much smaller than half the size of a burnt clay brick.

"You could have done this at the Capitol. Right out in the open. And then walked away."

"Possibly."

"You chose to rescue me instead, even though you claimed you didn't care what happened to me afterward. Another lie?"

"The virus," Carter said, ignoring the question. "The formula on there will help save lives?"

"Yes," she said. "Many more than last time."

"What if they'd gotten ahold of it?"

"Not as many lives would be saved. But a lot more money would be made. Which makes me glad you delivered it to me and not them."

"The invoice was clear," Carter said.

Dr. Zhang took another sip of tea. "So, what now?"

"You should contact the authorities. Let them know what happened. Otherwise we can't be sure you'll be safe."

"For a delivery guy, you're very concerned about my well-being."

"I try to avoid repeat trips, is all."

"Is that so?"

"I'd go with the FBI. No disrespect to the locals. It's more a resources thing. I can drop you off. It's on my way out of town."

"Why the rush? There's an excellent seafood place around the corner from my lab. My treat, once this is all over. It's the least I can do."

Black Hills National Forest and Custer State Park. That was it. Vice versa. Why did he have such a hard time remembering that?

"Ironically, I really am allergic," Carter said, putting the Suburban into drive. "But thanks anyway."

TROUBLE IS HIS BIZ

John H. Dromey

For many years, Gopher Hartman was the go-to guy for any overworked fellow private investigator who needed a gofer. Thus, his nickname, one (or more) might assume. One (or many) would be wrong. Gopher earned his moniker in grudging acknowledgement of his propensity for popping up in unexpected places, at unexpected times, as if from a hole in the ground. Sticking his neck out for a good cause was second nature to him.

Replete with details of his unconventional modus operandi, Gopher's casefiles were a revelation for anyone lucky enough to visit the inner sanctum of his out-of-the-way office.

A random example.

Gopher was hired to rid a golf course of a flock of pesky waterfowl, notorious for charging the greens in search of food and pecking the tees, wooden or plastic, with a vengeance. He assessed the situation and concluded the guilty parties were birds of a feather, or at least similar enough to be of the same avian family or genus or what have you.

The PI floated a number of possible remedies that did not get off the ground. The country club board of directors declined to stock the water hazards with alligators, piranhas, or the like. They were equally cool to the notion of getting all their ducks in a row prior to enlisting the aid of a sharpshooter known as a one-shot wonder. Without even a hint of irony, considering their location, the board cautioned Gopher not to make a hole in one, let alone in the whole bunch of birds. In other words, he must not reduce the flock with a Glock.

For someone of his mindset, failure was not an option. Briefly, he wondered if this case would be his swan song. Then, he remembered the saying *what's good for the goose is good for the gander*. Gopher recommended the installation of airport style noise makers—what's good for runways should be good for fairways—with a mulligan for anyone teeing off, or putting, whenever the devices were sounding. He was let go before learning whether or not his suggestion was adopted.

Either way, for him it was case closed. Gopher filed his notes in a manila folder labeled *The Maul-Tees Fowl Kin.*

There was no middle ground for Gopher. He tended to see everything as noir or blanc. Speaking in generalities with him was a waste of time for everyone concerned.

Before entrusting him with what I hoped would be a routine delivery of a valuable package, I wanted to make sure he was up to the task. I strove for specificity when I inquired about his health.

"Are you taking your blood pressure medicine?"

"No."

"Why not?"

"It's an Ace inhibitor."

"So?"

"I have a poker game every night this week."

"Are you on a winning streak?"

"Not exactly."

"Maybe skipping a night will improve your luck. Hear me out. At the very least, you can cut your losses. Not only that, you'll be able to earn some money at the same time."

"Is it a job you could do yourself?"

His question gave me pause. I feigned indifference the best way I knew how—I shrugged my shoulders. Then, I attempted to validate the contrived message of my body language with an offhand remark.

"I could, but I'd rather not. The errand requires meeting a client, after dark, in a part of town that's unfamiliar to me."

"I'll do it," Gopher said.

What a relief! I'd never been there, day or night, but I knew the district by its bad reputation. Gopher either didn't know or didn't care. I wasn't about to ask. All I knew was he'd be going where I feared to tread.

In the wee hours of the morning—standing on the crumbling sidewalk near the intersection of a mean street with a dark alley—Gopher Hartman, for perhaps the first time in his life, was unsure which way to turn. His uncharacteristic indecisiveness was cut short when somebody shot out the streetlight. After an additional moment's hesitation, the PI took an alternate route. Spotlighted by the broad beam of a flashlight, by all appearances, he went into cardiac arrest. He clutched his chest with crabbed fingers and slowly collapsed on the pavement.

The shaft of light bobbled about considerably before coming to rest on the PI's supine form. There was no discernible movement. A moment later, the light blinked off. The receding sound of feet pounding the pavement indicated two or more people were fleeing the scene. Apparently, they were afraid their culpability did not end with killing the light.

There was sufficient ambient illumination to reveal the contour of a dark figure emerging from the alley. The newcomer appeared to have all the time in the world as he crouched over the body. Whatever his intention, he not only took his time, he took a hands-on approach.

I caught up with Gopher a couple of days later. Other than having a facial expression sour enough to curdle powdered milk, he appeared to be none the worse for wear.

I tried to cheer him up by sharing my good news. "My client thought you were brilliant—playing possum the way you did."

"I had a panic attack."

"Call it what you will, your actions had the desired effect. Rather than risk being charged with felony murder during the commission of a crime, the would-be muggers ran away. My client retrieved his package intact. I've been paid in full, and I'm here to give you your share."

"I don't deserve it. I didn't get to the designated point of delivery on time. I fell short."

"That was a good thing. Otherwise, the muggers might have shot you both."

"They didn't, though."

"As far as I'm concerned, you earned your fee by serving as a decoy. Consider it hazardous duty pay. Were you hurt?"

The despondent PI put his right hand on his lower back. "I may have pulled a muscle in my lumbar region. I also have a bruise a little higher up. That's because your client tried to help me get to my feet, but his hand slipped and I fell backwards."

"That settles it. You deserve compensation for your injuries."

Gopher took the money. "There's just one problem," he said. "How am I going to write up this incident for my files?"

For most people, a pat answer like "you'll think of something" would do nicely. Not for Gopher. Fortunately, I'd been giving the matter some serious thought as we discussed the details of his recent assignment.

"Since there was a clever deception involved, and—despite the lethal potential in your predicament—you survived, you might want to adapt a detail from the chronicles of Sherlock Holmes. Namely, you can designate your latest case as *My Close Calls with Wreckin'-Back Falls*."

GATOR BAIT

DG Critchley

A number of street-level dealers had been disappearing in Miami over the last year or so. Miami Dade cops weren't particularly concerned about fewer dealers on the street. Still, missing dealers were reported across Broward County as well. Fort Lauderdale police had asked the FBI to determine if it was an unusually tidy turf war or something else, like a vigilante. And that's how I, Travis Tredman, your friendly neighborhood FBI Special Agent, ended up waist-deep in the Everglades looking for anything remotely resembling a clue.

The latest disappearance was a charming gentleman named Ralph Carolli. Mr. Carolli was a notorious crime figure, at least according to Mr. Carolli. The truth was that Ralphie was a bottom-feeder, a street-level drug dealer, and about as subtle as a kick in the teeth. The Miami-Dade cops were well aware that Ralphie Carolli wasn't using his van to deliver hot meals to orphanages. But, despite the fact he was dumber than a box of hammers, the cops couldn't figure out who his supplier was. So he kept "slipping through their fingers." Ralphie thought he was a criminal mastermind. Most of his associates considered it dumb luck, with the emphasis on dumb. In truth, Miami Dade PD kept him on the streets, hoping the idiot would lead them up the supply chain.

The question was further complicated when Ralphie disappeared. His van was found along the Tamiami Trail with a nail in a tire. Since this was inside Big Cypress National Preserve, it became a Federal issue. The FBI office in Naples technically had jurisdiction, but they were more than happy to dump the case on the Miami office. And like so many other viscous substances, swamp water flows downhill to the desk of the agent with the least seniority. And that would be me.

The Big Cypress park ranger that had found the van was standing watch on the edge of the road with a rifle in case of alligators. It was not giving me a particularly warm fuzzy feeling. I would note that Ranger Wilson was also a drop-dead gorgeous blonde, but I have found it a wise choice to avoid making observations that could be construed as sexist by heavily armed women.

I spotted something glinting in the sun. I slogged over and gingerly lifted a small plastic bag floating on the water. It was filled with white powder. I looked around. There was nothing else to be seen.

I climbed back onto dry land and fought my way out of my government-issued hip waders. Ranger Wilson put the rifle away and started the Jeep. I bagged the evidence, and we drove back to the ranger station on a dirt trail of dubious quality.

"So, Agent Tredman, what's the next step?" She was driving at speeds I would not have been comfortable with, even if the road had been paved.

I struck a casual pose, hoping my internal organs didn't shift around too much from the jarring they were enduring. "I'm not sure. Ralphie isn't the first dealer who's vanished. If we're lucky, that bag was coke, but I'll let the lab deal with that. Sometimes we can pinpoint the dealer by the composition. Maybe if we know who we're looking for, some of the pieces will fall into place."

She nodded. We pulled into the ranger station, and I transferred to my car and headed back to the FBI office in Miramar on real, paved roads.

Getting back to the office, I signed the bag over to the lab and went to see my boss, Special Agent-in-Charge Alberto Fernández Duhalde.

He seemed interested in the powder I sent to the lab. "Tredman, did you happen to examine the powder?"

I shook my head. "I really don't have much field experience in drug interdiction."

He stood up and headed out toward the lab. I shrugged and followed him.

"Dr. Daniels, may I take a quick look at that evidence Agent Tredman dropped off?"

Dr. Daniels looked mildly annoyed and unlocked the evidence cabinet. He handed the evidence bag to Duhalde. He pulled out the plastic bag and undid the twist tie. He carefully sniffed at the opening and smiled.

He held it toward me. "Tredman, what do you smell?"

I carefully sniffed. "Oranges?"

He nodded, sealed the bag, and handed it back to the scientist, and we headed back toward his office.

"Chief, what is that bag?" I was puzzled.

He didn't break stride. "Oh, it's definitely cocaine."

I was no less puzzled. "Doesn't coke usually smell like nail polish remover?"

We stepped into his office. "Yes. The cocaine picks up the smell from whatever solvent was used to dissolve the base. When the dealer washes the cocaine with acetone, it smells of acetone—nail polish remover."

He motioned me to sit down. I couldn't help but notice his office was the only place in the building that was adequately air-conditioned.

"Fortunately, since cocaine picks up the scent of any solvent it's washed in, we can sometimes identify the manufacturer by the scent. The lab boys think the citrus smell means it was washed with limonene, a solvent produced from citrus oil. And there's only one person in south Florida whose coke has that fresh citrusy scent—Eduardo Valencia."

He pulled a file out of a pile and slid it across his desk. "Congratulations. You're now the FBI liaison on an inter-agency task force trying to nail Fast Eddie Valencia. Officially it's because your missing dealer connects the two cases. Unofficially, you're replacing me because if I have to directly deal with that collection of idiot middle-management desk jockeys any longer, there will be gunplay."

I picked up the file. It was not a thin folder.

"That's not the entire file, Tredman, and don't waste a lot of time reading it. It's mostly inter-agency posturing. Basically, Valencia is an up-and-coming star in drug circles. If you can think of a federal agency, he's on their radar. The problem is some of those same middle management pencil pushers at the USDA banned Colombian citrus imports a couple of years back because someone saw an insect they thought was something else. Colombia didn't import a lot of citrus. Still, the ban made the produce wholesalers down there switch to orange juice and processed products. It happened so fast that no one has a clear idea of how many citrus plants are still in operation down there or where the by-products are going."

I tapped the folder. "So someone is cooking coke with this limonene solvent and smuggling it into Florida."

Duhalde nodded. "If we nail this guy, we send a message to the rest of the lowlife and embarrass a lot of Federal agencies that seem to need a reminder that we're the FBI."

I walked back to my desk and started thumbing through the file. The boss was right. Most of it was meeting notes. From the looks of it, the committee was more concerned with who got credit for the bust. The rest of the file was all conjecture—psych profiles, projected drug routes—anything and everything except for an actual plan to track down Fast Eddie Valencia. It was late afternoon when I finally finished. I stood up to leave when Duhalde's door opened, and he gestured me in.

"Tredman, I may have made a tactical error." He didn't look particularly upset about it. "I called the DEA agent in charge of the task force to tell him you were now the FBI representative."

The phone buzzed. He picked it up and listened. "Okay, send her up."

He hung up and sighed. "The good news is I didn't mention why you're on the committee. The bad news is I did mention where we found Ralphie Carolli's van. The task force, in its infinite wisdom, has decided that since Mr. Carolli was found in Big Cypress, the National Park Service should also join the fun."

There was a knock on the door, and Ranger Wilson walked in. Duhalde stood up. "Agent Tredman, I believe you know Ranger Jennifer Wilson?"

I nodded, eyeing the holstered gun dangling off one hip. Hers was bigger than mine.

Ranger Wilson will be working with you on the case and will represent the Park Service on the joint task force. If we can get the NWS and the USGS involved, we'll hold the record for the largest inter-agency operation with no results. The closest they've come to success is having J-CODE leave the task force.

Ranger Wilson looked at me blankly. "J-CODE?"

I nodded. "We're the FBI. We love anagrams. J-CODE is 'Joint Criminal Opioid and Darknet Enforcement.' If they left the task force, it means there's no evidence Fast Eddie is using the darknet to move his drugs."

The ranger looked less than enlightened. "I spend most of my waking hours in a swamp. What's a darknet, and who's Fast Eddie?"

Duhalde politely cleared his throat. "Tredman, bring Ranger Wilson up to speed. Preferably not in my office. Officially, you are to share all information and cooperate fully with the joint task force. Unofficially, use your own discretion—these idiots can't even agree where to buy doughnuts for their next meeting. Just be careful. Fast Eddie is a nasty customer and aggressively expanding his operations."

The phone buzzed again. He picked it up and shooed us out with his hand.

Ranger Wilson looked at me as we walked back to my desk. "I haven't eaten since this morning. Is there a bodega nearby where I can grab a sandwich?"

"Actually, neither have I. The boss said to bring you up to speed. That sounds like I can expense a real meal. Unfortunately, the closest thing to a real meal around here is a pizza joint around the corner. We can go over the case there."

She looked concerned. "In a pizzeria? What about being overheard?"

You're in uniform with a sidearm. I am obviously FBI in this suit. Do you really think anyone would even think of sitting near us?"

She paused. "Okay, pizza it is. Do you need to call your husband?"

I looked at her. "My husband? I don't have a husband!"

She shrugged. "Okay, boyfriend."

I stared at her. "I am not gay."

She shrugged again. "Fine, my mistake. Call your girlfriend."

"I don't have one of those either." I realized my teeth were clenched.

It went downhill from there. The pizza was New York style, which to a New Englander like me, is as much an anathema as Manhattan clam chowder. Even worse, Ranger Wilson was a vegetarian, so she wouldn't eat meat, and I won't eat mushrooms. So we had pizza, plain and boring.

I went over what we knew. "Fast Eddie was a Colombian national who showed up out of nowhere about two years ago and forced his way into the Miami drug markets with a great deal of large-caliber persuasion. DEA can't figure out who his supplier is in South America. Coast Guard, TSA, Border Patrol—nobody has ever intercepted any of his shipments. The Bureau of International Narcotics has nothing in South America. The FBI is working on the theory that the coke is being shipped to Europe and then back to Miami. All that's certain is that he's ruthless and expanding his territory with extreme prejudice. At current rates, he'll control most of the South Florida drug trade in another year or so."

The ranger listened. "So why not lock him up?"

I shrugged. "Knowing something and proving it in court are two different matters. As far as the evidence shows, Eduardo Valencia is the owner and CEO of Tastee Sunshine Foods, a successful wholesale food distributor specializing in fresh dairy products. We have nothing to connect him to the drugs."

She picked at her pizza crusts. "So why am I involved?"

I shrugged. "I don't know. I think the task force is so incompetent that they keep adding agencies in hopes that someone will trip over a way to catch Fast Eddie. My suggestion to you is to find some unavoidable project in the morning that makes it impossible to attend the task force."

I signaled for the bill. She poked at the crusts again. "Agent Tredman, may I ask an odd question?"

"Yes, I'm sure I'm not gay."

"No, why are you here, in Florida? It's obvious you don't like being here."

I handed my credit card to the waiter. "I requested a transfer to the Miami office after a bad break-up in Boston. I'm assuming it was a break-up since she never told me she had moved to Hawaii to live off the grid with some insanely good-looking, muscular Adonis-type. Miami has turned out to be equally disappointing—hot, humid, and nothing like what I would have expected based on Miami Vice reruns."

She grimaced. "Ouch."

I signed the slip and stood up. "Let me ask you a question. Why did you think I was gay? Is it these shoes? Because it's really hard to find shoes that are comfortable and still match these dark suits."

We walked back to the FBI offices. "No, the shoes are fine. Your tie, however, is positively horrible. I assumed you were gay because of this afternoon. The Park Service has worked with other law enforcement agencies. Sooner or later, some badge-wearing ape makes a crack about my figure or how well my uniform fits. My favorite is how I'm 'too pretty to be carrying such a big gun.' You were polite, professional, and not a crack about how I'd look prettier with make-up."

I nodded. "The Boston Police Department felt that way about my ex-girlfriend's ass. It didn't seem to matter that she was a Harvard professor and a top expert in her field."

We stopped at her Jeep. "Now I understand. You're just a nice guy. No wonder you screwed up my gaydar."

It got awkward quiet. Finally, I said, "Good night, Ranger. Seriously, consider having a conflict on your calendar in the morning to skip the meeting."

She nodded. "I will. Good night Agent Tredman."

I considered going back into the office. I went home instead.

The following day, Duhalde was waiting when I walked in the door. It has been my experience that the boss waiting for you never ends well.

"Tredman, in my office, please." Bosses saying please also never boded well. I followed him in. He sat down. I decided to keep standing.

"I'll give you credit, Tredman. When you find an excuse to skip a task force meeting, you go big."

I stood there. I hadn't skipped the meeting—it wasn't due to start until 11, so I had plenty of time to head into Miami.

Duhalde continued. "Ranger Wilson called the office this morning. The ranger was out in the swamp, looking around where they found Mr. Carolli's van. She found a clue and wants you to head to the ranger station as soon as possible."

Now I was concerned. "Did I miss something?"

Duhalde shook his head. "No. Mr. Carolli just needed an extra day to float to the surface."

I wasn't sure if I was relieved or sickened. "She found Ralphie?"

He paused. "Well, she found most of him. The good ranger came across an alligator having a snack on what was left of Mr. Carolli. The alligator was disinclined to share, so Ranger Wilson was forced to put a bullet into its brain with great accuracy."

I turned to head out the door. I'll be out in Big Cypress.

Duhalde stopped me. "Tredman, Mr. Carolli is being brought to our morgue. I assume the cause of death will not be natural. She wants you to review the necropsy on the alligator."

I stopped. "I have no idea what I'd be looking at—I'm not a veterinarian."

Duhalde nodded. "True, but if you're investigating a lead, you can't attend a useless task force meeting. More importantly, are you going to argue with a woman who just took out a 7-foot alligator with one bullet?"

The Big Cypress research facilities were on the Tamiami Trail in Ochopee, a 90-minute drive from Miramar. I flashed my badge to a rather unpleasant-looking ranger at the desk who made a call. Ranger Wilson came out to the lobby wearing a surgical mask.

"Thanks, Edkins." Ranger Unhappy Face merely shrugged.

"I hear you had some luck hunting this morning, Ranger Wilson." What does one say as a greeting to a surgical mask?

Her eyes furrowed. "I hate killing alligators, but evidence is evidence. Call me Jenn if we're going to be working together. I'll call you Travis."

I shook my head. "I prefer Tredman. I was named after a relative I don't like."

She handed me a surgical mask. "You'll want this, Tredman. The inside of an alligator is not a bed of flowers."

We walked into a small room of metal cabinets and tables. The smell was all but incapacitating, a combination of vomit, ammonia, urine, and a hint of formaldehyde. It definitely was not the next big thing in perfumes, but sadly, not the worst I had encountered. A woman in full surgical scrubs was hunched over, examining the inside of what I assumed was our alligator. She saw us and straightened up.

"Just in time, Jennifer. This is the 'definitely not gay' FBI guy you mentioned?"

I stuck a hand out to shake, noticed the bloody gloves, and waved instead. "Special Agent Travis Tredman, FBI."

"Regina Yáñez, DVM. Jennifer has given me a good one."

I wasn't sure what constituted a "good one" in terms of an alligator with its internal organs spread out on a metal table, but the vet seemed pretty pleased. She gestured to a tray on the counter. I could see at least one part I could recognize—a human hand.

Dr. Yáñez glanced at the tray. "Stomach contents are one male left hand and several unidentified chunks of flesh and muscle. All human, but based on skin tones, there are at least three different victims involved, two Caucasians or light-skinned

Latinos, and one African-American."

"So that's not Ralphie's hand?" All I knew about Ralphie was he was a chubby little short guy with questionable personal hygiene habits but Caucasian.

Jenn was standing as far away from the gator as possible. "No. The alligator was working on a leg. Your dealer had both hands when the coroner picked up the remains. I guess you guys will need to run prints on this hand."

"So, the alligator is a man-eater?" I still wasn't sure if Ralphie's demise as an alligator's brunch was relevant to the case or just really bad luck.

Yáñez shrugged. "Technically, yes, but this is odd. Alligators prefer smaller animals they can grab and eat with a single bite. To kill larger prey, they have to grab it and dragging it underwater to drown."

Jenn spoke up from the corner. "If an alligator grabbed your friend Ralphie and drowned him, the autopsy will confirm it. An alligator won't normally eat something bigger than one bite until it rots enough to be easy to tear."

Yáñez tapped the tray of human parts with her scalpel. "If the meat is still too fresh, the alligator will grab a mouthful and spin around until a bite-sized piece is ripped off. These parts are shredded. This gator was ripping meat off in wildly varied sizes. Combined with superficial wounds on the exterior hide, our scaly friend here was regularly fighting for his share of dinner."

"So, there's a pack of man-eating alligators wandering around the swamps?" It seemed like a bad thing for tourism but still not relevant to Fast Eddie.

"Technically, a congregation," Jenn spoke up. She was still in the far corner, which I noticed was directly under the air vent.

"What?" I wondered if there was room for two near the vent.

"A group of alligators is a congregation, not a pack," she said.

The doc tapped a scalpel on the tray. "If you two are done arguing semantics."

We both looked at her. She put the scalpel down and picked up the severed hand. "The wrist of this hand shows perimortem bruising."

Even I knew what that meant. The guy who formerly owned that hand was alive and still attached to it when the gator grabbed it.

Yáñez put the hand back on the tray. "The weirdness just keeps getting weirder." She gestured at the alligator parts across her table. "The gator was on borrowed time. He had a blockage in his intestines. It appears to be a mass of small plastic bags."

Now I was interested.

The doc continued. "And, the weirdest of all, this gator had ischemic vascular disease, specifically coronary arteriosclerosis."

"In English, Doc?" I think I recognized a couple of words.

She looked at me. "The gator had clogged arteries."

"Is that even possible?" Jenn came over to the carcass.

"Normally, I'd say no. He's probably not a smoker. I haven't checked his blood sugar, but I doubt he had diabetes either."

Jenn seemed puzzled. "So, how does that even happen?"

Finally, a question I could answer. "It's cocaine. Clogged arteries are a side effect of long-term coke use."

They both looked at me. "Small plastic bags? Spare body parts? Clogged arteries? The alligator has been eating my missing dealers."

They looked at each other. In horror, I realized what I had to do next.

"Doc, Can I smell those plastic bags?"

It was her turn to look puzzled. "Excuse me?"

"I need to determine if they smell like citrus." I assumed my total lack of enthusiasm was evident.

She looked at me. "I would assume they smell like an alligator's intestinal tract."

I sighed. "Humor me, Doc. I didn't say I was looking forward to it."

She tossed me a pair of rubber gloves and gestured toward a metal tray. I detected a faint whiff of citrus on two of the bags before my sinuses shut down completely. If the FBI wanted to check the rest, they were on their own.

Yáñez stood there, watching the tears roll down my face. I would bet she was grinning under that mask. Gator innards are nasty, plain and simple.

Finally, she said. "Hate to break this to you, but I was planning on running everything through our gas chromatography equipment. We do a lot of forensics on wildlife in case of pesticide poisoning."

I nodded, still trying to avoid swallowing. "Your equipment can verify it's cocaine with traces of limonene. That's all I need for now, except for some fresh air."

Ranger Edkins didn't look any happier to see me leaving. Agent Wilson strolled out after me. "Doc likes you. She thinks you're funny."

I ignored her. "Can you show me a map of where you found Ralphie?"

She ducked back inside and came out with a rolled map. She spread out a topographic map on the hood of my car and studied it.

Then she pointed down. "Right there." She traced a line through the green. "That's the Tamiami Trail. The yellow-brown lines are ranger access roads. What are you looking for, Tredman?"

"I'm wondering if Fast Eddie has set up shop along the Tamiami, and he's feeding people to alligators as a way to dispose of the competition. That gators have started associating the citrus smell of his cocaine with a free dinner. When Ralphie blew a tire, he must have sampled the product. The gator caught the scent and came for lunch. But there are no buildings or side roads near where you found Ralphie's remains."

She looked at the map. "You're not a local—When the Federal Reserve came in, there were businesses all along the Tamiami. There are still a couple of quarries grandfathered in and a couple of wildlife parks and hunt clubs. And abandoned roads with abandoned buildings don't all appear on the maps. What exactly are you thinking?"

I stared at the map. "I don't know. Limonene is a solvent produced from citrus oil. Maybe an old chemical warehouse?"

"Citrus? How about an abandoned orange juice factory?" She looked at the map again. "And it's only a mile or so from where I found your buddy."

"It's too far away. What are the odds that alligator would find Ralphie?" I looked at the map, hoping for a bright red arrow pointing to a clue.

Jenn looked at me. "Here's a little trivia fact for you—alligators have a keen sense of smell. That gator could have easily smelled that citrusy cocaine from a mile away."

She looked at me. I pulled my gun and checked the clip. "It's worth a shot. I'll update the boss, and we'll take a look before I see if we need to call in the cavalry."

My phone couldn't find a signal. Jenn watched. "There's a reason we still use radios—there's no cell service in most of the Everglades—it's not exactly a high traffic area. And before you ask, our landline is down again."

I hadn't even thought of landline telephones. Ranger Jenn looked at the sky. "We have four hours of good light left. And I do not want to be wandering around an abandoned building in the Everglades once it starts getting dark."

I made a decision. "So, we either go now, or we drive east until I can get a signal just to tell my boss we're looking at an empty building that is probably an empty building."

She nodded. "I'll have Edkins radio our HQ, and they can let the FBI know what we're doing. How's that?"

I nodded. She ducked back in and then came out with a rifle. She put it on the gun rack next to the other one. "Edkins agreed, without a fight. Apparently, he likes you too. Let's go play in the swamp."

I got into the Jeep. "Ranger Wilson, never let it be said you're not a fun date."

She snorted as she gunned the engine. "Absolutely. But next time, try chocolates instead of a coked-up alligator."

We went roaring down dirt roads again and then pulled on to the Tamiami. She was still hitting speeds that I considered excessive, but at least it was straight and paved this time.

"So," I said, hoping to distract her just enough to slow down, "Why is there an orange juice factory in the middle of the Everglades?"

Jenn switched lanes to go whipping past a state police patrol car. They just waved. I assumed they knew when to pick their fights.

She glanced in the rearview mirror for a split second. "From what they tell me, the factory was built with the idea that they could truck fruit from the groves on both coasts by building between them. Then they could ship the juice to either coast as needed. It lasted for about four years. 1962 was the worst hard freeze on record, doing more damage to the orange trees than any hurricane. The company failed, the property was seized for back taxes, and Park Service is letting the building go back to the swamp."

We suddenly turned left into a roadside parking area, just a gravel parking lot and a boardwalk for nature lovers. She scanned the parking lot and drove over to a padlocked metal gate marked "restricted access." We got out of the Jeep. I looked beyond the gate. All I saw was an old dirt road that continued beyond a copse of mangrove trees. Jenn was staring at the gate. I looked and saw nothing odd.

"Tredman, we may be on to something after all." She grabbed the padlock. "This isn't one of our locks."

"You have a brand?"

She let the lock drop again. "Park Service is Federal too. This is not the manufacturer with the government contract. Somebody's using their own lock."

Jen pulled a pair of binoculars out of the Jeep and hopped the gate. "Coming?"

Wordlessly, I climbed over the fence. We walked quickly to the mangroves and gazed down the road. Even without the binoculars, I could see that building was in surprisingly good shape for a factory supposedly being reclaimed by nature. She handed me the glasses.

The parking lot had a Tastee Sunshine Foods van parked by the door, and there were three men outside the entrance, expensively dressed, each toting an AK-47. Unless the local alligator poachers were having a formal dress event, I think we found Fast Eddie's distribution center.

She motioned, and we went back to the Jeep. She pulled both rifles out and tossed one to me. "Congratulations Tredman, this is officially the worst date ever."

I checked the rifle and rechecked my very puny-looking service revolver. "So, next time, I go with the chocolates?"

"If we live, you better make it dinner at a place with tablecloths and real silverware."

I knew I had no cell reception in the middle of a swamp, but I checked anyway. Jenn radioed her office and told Edkins to contact my boss with details and directions.

We were going to need backup, preferably a Miami SWAT team. I'd prefer a battalion or two of Marines, but I don't think USMC was currently on the task force.

"What now, Ranger Wilson?"

She shook her head. "We might be able to pick off the three outside guards, but we don't know how many are inside. So, I suggest reconnaissance until the cavalry arrives."

We crept forward to a lonely-looking cypress tree, which looked more promising than sitting in the sawgrass. We had just settled down against the tree when the three goons all looked at their phones at the same time.

Jen saw it too. "Somebody has Wi-Fi in their drug den."

The three of them looked a lot more alert and started to look more intently at the flora.

"They know we're out here," I said, stating the obvious.

"But how?"

I knew. "The same way Fast Eddie knew there was a building off the Tamiami that no one was using. Probably the same person in the Park Service who's supposed to have been checking the structure."

Jen looked grim. "Edkins. And he's the only one who knows where we are."

I glanced at the rifle. "We're not getting any backup." I was stating the obvious again.

As if on cue, a Park Service Jeep pulled up to the building, and our buddy Edkins jumped out and went into the building.

I watched the three nattily dressed thugs continue to scan the underbrush. "What now? We were already outnumbered and outgunned. And they know we're out here."

Jen cradled the rifle, "We separate and head back to the Jeep. The first one there uses the radio to get help."

I shook my head. "And if Edkins has any sense, he destroyed the radio in your Jeep when he unlocked the gate."

Jen did not look happy. I knew the feeling. "Then the first one back to the Jeep heads back to the station and uses the emergency radio."

I looked at her. "No, Jen. You need to go. I can't possibly remember those dirt roads back to your base. I'll stay here and create a diversion."

She kissed me on the cheek. "You really are a good guy. Try to survive our first date. I'll handle details for the next one."

"Next one?"

She smiled. "Think of it as a reason to live."

She disappeared into the brush. I decided to go around to one of the sides of the building with fewer AK-47s. The FBI would have a helluva an expense report if I lived because the Everglades were wreaking havoc on my imported Italian shoes.

Something splashed in front of me, and it sounded bigger than a wading bird. An alligator was traveling toward the building at a speed I had been very comfortable not knowing alligators could achieve. More followed the first. The dinosaurs all congregated by a loading dock. I looked behind the building. Almost invisible in the swamplands, a greenhouse stretched out into the wetlands. Suddenly the loading dock door rolled up, and Ranger Edkins was unceremoniously tossed out. I couldn't smell citrus, but I'd bet those alligators did. Edkins screamed as the alligators converged on him. It was a short scream. The alligators fought over the remains as the door rolled shut again. The alligators stayed. I guess they could still smell the limonene.

Suddenly I heard a noise behind me—the unforgettable sound of an AK47 being cocked.

"Excuse me, officer, but my boss would like a word with you."

I stood up. He took my revolver and the rifle. We quietly walked down to the building. The other two thugs just glared and followed him inside. Catching the stupid FBI agent was obviously worth extra points with the boss.

I was marched up to a man reading a clipboard. He wore a suit that cost more than my car, even assuming I had bought it new.

He looked up. "Hello, Mr. FBI agent."

I tried to look less terrified than I was. "Special Agent Travis Tredman, FBI. I'd offer to show you my credentials, but I assume your associates with the AK-47s would frown at my placing my hand in my jacket."

He laughed. His teeth were blinding white and perfect. Drug lords must have had a better dental plan than the FBI.

"Mr. Valencia, I presume?"

He nodded. "Si. A pleasure to meet you, Agent Tredman." He barked something in Spanish, and two goons went back out the door. The third guy stood a respectful distance away, but with the AK-47 pointed disrespectfully at me.

I assessed the situation; even I wasn't putting odds on my survival, and I was considered the optimistic one. It was a corrugated tin building, two-stories with small windows along the upper walls. In the late 1950s, it was cheap ventilation. Half hidden among the support beams and shadows, a questionably stable catwalk provided access to the windows. I assumed the options were open or closed. There was no way I'd get up there and out a window with the amount of firepower in the room. The floor was cement, so I wasn't tunneling out. The front door had the AK-47 twins. The loading dock garage door was padlocked, and the door next to it led to the same place: the all-you-can-eat buffet for alligators.

I decided the best plan that didn't involve a horrible death trying to outrun alligators and/or high-velocity bullets was to use my boyish charm and stall.

"I assume I'm alive because you need an inside man to replace the one your pets just ate." I hoped it sounded casual, but that's hard to fake with an assault rifle pointed at you.

Fast Eddie put the clipboard on a crate. "Agent Tredman, you cut me to the quick. Alligators are magnificent wild creatures. Although I do feed them, it is out of admiration, not as trained pets. The late Ranger Edkins chose to disobey my orders and came here, risking his value to my business. So he was given a new assignment."

I glanced toward the loading dock. "And his new assignment was to serve as a distraction so your men could sneak up on the idiot FBI agent."

He smiled again with those flawless pearly white teeth. "I merely multi-task whenever it is possible." If I lived, I was going to shoot his dentist.

I shrugged. "It is hard to argue with efficiency."

He laughed again, showing his teeth were white all the way back. He probably had his wisdom teeth bleached as well, on the remote chance they needed to come out.

"Agent Tredman, I like you." The smile was a little more ominous. "But I have other associates who happen to work in the public sector. You're really not a strong recruitment candidate."

"So I'm gator bait." I was stating the obvious again.

"Crudely put, but yes, eventually." He smiled again, but it was not a happy smile.

"Eventually?" I had taken a casual step toward the gun pointed at me. Another 4-5 steps, and I might be in "desperate lunge for the gun" range. No luck. Gun-boy immediately took a step backward, maintaining his distance. Apparently, he was familiar with the "desperate lunge for the gun" trick.

Fast Eddie smiled this time with no pretense of warmth. "I know you're on the task force, so you're going to tell me everything you know."

I looked at him dumbfounded. "Really? I've been on the task force for less than 24 hours. You must really be generous with your bribes!"

Fast Eddie smiled, and this time it was sincere. I fantasized about knocking those enameled abominations out of his mouth.

"So," I started cautiously, "the longer I talk, the longer I live?"

The smile tightened a little. Good for me. "Agent Tredman, you are an optimist. You're thinking that pretty little park ranger is going to get help and rescue you."

I shrugged. "The thought had crossed my mind."

Fast Eddie's face reminded me of a cat I had growing up. It loved to play with its prey until death was actually a blessing. I almost expected him to purr.

Still wearing a charmless smile, he looked at me. "Ranger Edkins, before his recent accident, was quite efficient. He removed the radio from your vehicle. So the señorita will have to drive back to the warden station, only to discover that, by an unfortunate coincidence, the base radio and phone are both out of service. So, she will need to seek help much farther away. I do not believe you can talk that long."

He smiled broadly again with the gleaming white teeth. The AK-47 was the only reason I didn't consider trying to knock them out of his mouth.

So I talked. Like my boss said, most of the file was useless, but there were a lot of pages. I could see he was getting bored. And even I knew a bored drug lord equaled a dead FBI agent. I started trying to think of lies that would sound like facts in a government file. I happened to glance over his shoulder.

I stopped reciting the theories on how the drugs were arriving. "You're not smuggling them into the country—you're making them here!"

He flashed those damned pearly white teeth again and glanced over at what I saw—a greenhouse door was open, and the greenhouse was full of shrubs with red berries. It was either holly or coca plants, and I had already decided Fast Eddie was not Santa Claus.

"Rico, shut that door." AK-47 strolled over to shut the door.

Fast Eddie shrugged. "It's hard enough to grow coca this far north without the staff leaving the greenhouse open."

A shot rang out, and Rico dropped like a rock. Fast Eddie turned and pulled a pistol out of his belt.

Mama Tredman didn't raise any idiots. I ran the other way, ducking behind a large mixing vat. I assessed the situation. No weapon, no backup, and the presumably deceased henchman was too far out in the open to make a run for his weapon. The vat was full of coke paste, waiting for a solvent bath. Four or five small barrels of limonene were stacked on the wall. The labels suggested they'd been here since the 1960s. Fast Eddie was frugal too.

Eddie was trying to spot the shooter. Other than a wooden mixing paddle, I could not see anything that could inflict significant bodily harm on Fast Eddie, and I suspect I'd be dead long before I could paddle him to death.

I saw another shot and a flash of khaki and blonde hair. Jen Wilson. She was on a catwalk and running out of places to go. Fast Eddie knew it too. He fired a shot and waited until she reached the end of the catwalk.

He slowly took aim. I grabbed a barrel of limonene and tossed it. It landed with a crash. He turned to look. Jen took the opportunity to fire. She missed again but hit the barrel. It starting spilling across the floor. I tried to remember the properties of limonene. I knew it was a skin and eye irritant. That gave me an idea. I grabbed another barrel and popped off the lid. As soon as Jen fired again, I rushed out and heaved the barrel's contents over Fast Eddie. Eddie took a bath in limonene, face-first. With a scream of pain, he dropped to his knees and started firing blindly.

The first shot grazed my ribs and knocked the wind out of me. The next shot ricocheted off an electric heating unit on the mixing vat. The sparks hit the limonene, and it ignited. I suddenly remembered that limonene was also flammable. It started to spread quickly. I tried to help Fast Eddie get up. He struggled to his feet and fought me off. Then clutching an empty gun, he blindly staggered toward the nearest door—the one out to the loading dock.

"Jen, get the hell out here." I charged toward the front door. She jumped down the ladder, and we ran outside.

"Your drug lord is escaping!"

"He just ran out the door where a congregation of alligators is trained to eat anything with a citrus smell." I could already hear the shrieks.

"Why are we still running?"

"Fun fact I remembered recently. Limonene is not only flammable, it also forms an explosive vapor."

"Oh, crap."

The building exploded. Smoking corrugated debris had stopped raining down as we reached the Jeep.

She turned and kissed me. "Definitely the worst first date ever."

"Remind me to tell you about my first date with the ex in Boston. I was hospitalized for four weeks. Say, aren't you supposed to be off getting help?"

"Edkins was too efficient. He disabled the Jeep as well as the radio. So I doubled back and tried his radio. There was no reply, so I assume he took out the radio at the station. Since I was there, I decided to take a look around and used their own Wi-Fi to call for backup."

"What about the two clowns with A-47s at the door?"

She just smiled. I decided I didn't want to know. I glanced at the plume of smoke and suddenly felt light-headed. Somewhere in a distant echo chamber, Ranger Wilson said something about me being shot, which I knew already. Then I heard a helicopter. Duhalde was pulling out the stops. Which was good, because I suddenly didn't feel very well ...

I woke up in a hospital with Jen sitting by the bed and a strong case of déjà vu from my days in the Boston office. I decided I could live with that, but it would be a long time before I could stand the smell of citrus again. Naturally, my boss then strolled in with a gift basket of oranges.

Eduardo "Fast Eddie" Valencia remains a fugitive from justice, at least as far as Miami-Dade and Federal Law Enforcement Officials are concerned. No body was found in the debris, but I know better. Fast Eddie will never be found unless some trapper finds some unnaturally white teeth in a pile of alligator scat.

MURDER BY THE SEA

Jennifer Steil

Marina stands looking at the patch of dawn flickering on the remaining sea. So small, so far. You couldn't get too close to the water anymore or the sand would take you. It holds her sinking feet too tightly and she lets it. She deserves to be held here, at the scene of the crime. It's only fair. They had taken the sea, piece by piece. They had turned it this way and that, strangled the rivers that fed it, poured it over the mouths of thirsty cotton.

When she was a girl, she had thought it would crash to these Karakalpak shores her whole life, through her grandchildren's lives. None of them had made plans for when it left and their town, their lively sea town, became a stretch of brown, stinking sand that now did no thing at all. The mushrooms she loved disappeared from riverbanks. Salted soil spoiled the cotton, withered the almond and apple trees behind their homes. Chemical dust filled the lungs of their children. The sun burned nearly every drop of pristine water into thin air.

She bends to curl her fingers around a plastic water bottle. A near lifetime ago, her fingers had cleaned scales from fish. When their bodies began turning up rotting and poisoned, and her husband Sergei had gone to work on the island and never returned, not even when the island was no longer an island but part of the shore, when the Russians in a panic razed it all to rubble, she had left, traveled far from Mo'ynoq, stayed away for years. In Tashkent, she cleaned a house that rarely needed cleaning, a house without crusted salt and mud. She washed clothing that still smelled of soap from the last wash.

Retired now, returned, she spends most of her time sleeping in a yurt hours north of the town. She watches the water; she keeps vigil. She no longer has to clean. But cleaning becomes habit, so she cleans the sand. She tends the shores of what remains. She cannot clean poisons from the waters but she can do this. She has become housekeeper to the sea.

She is stuffing the bottle into her woolen sack when she sees something larger down the sand. Something longer and manlike. As she steps closer, the muck clutching at her heels like a child trying to keep a parent from leaving, she sees his silver hair, his round belly, the familiar bend of his nose. Yusup, husband of her daughter, the daughter named Darya for the river.

Drunk again, she thinks. That's why he never made it back to the yurt last night, not that any of them had stayed up waiting.

On the wet sand nearby she sees the shell of a drink, the drink they now had in place of the sea. The drink that took the pain and turned it numb. They poured and toasted what they'd killed, as if the crime were not theirs. As if inebriate incantations could make it rise once more.

"Wake up, fool." She nudges his ribs with a calloused toe, but his body just rocks in the sand, stiff. She reaches for his heart, to listen for it with her palm, cries out in sharp shock. Something nearly invisible protrudes from his chest. Glass. She rubs a bleeding hand against her jeans. She touches the glass again, careful this time, sees the Qara of Qarataw on the shard. Vodka: the only pristine liquid they have left. Qarataw has killed many men, but not like this.

She can't pretend sorrow. She never liked her daughter's husband. Darya too had come to despise him, especially after he started with that fungicide business. But who liked their husbands here? What was left of them to like? Maybe Mo'ynoq once had good men, when they could spend the day in the water and return with gleaming sturgeon, pike perch, or trout. But who can love a husband who is home all day and thinks cleaning is beneath him? Marina was lucky to be widowed young. Once there were tigers here, lush forests, and foxes. Once there were men.

She walks back up the hill, past more bottles half buried in mud and sand, plastic bags tied tight, trash telling them how they still don't learn. The wind is cold and the dirt not the kind the earth makes but the kind humans make, the kind that reflects no light.

When she returns, rolling up the carpet from the doorway and tying it fast, she finds Darya alone with baby Saiga. Everyone in her family named for something that no longer thrives. Darya's shoulders sag in relief when Marina tells her.

"But it wasn't me," she says. "You don't think I would, do you?"

Marina shrugs. So many people do things you don't think they would. She hadn't thought her husband would marry their daughter off to a man who would sell fungicides to farmers whose land was already poisoned. Whose sole ambition was forgetfulness. She looks up at the beams of willow, the only wood that bends enough to form shelter, then out at her granddaughter Tethys, raised on sour camel milk and bread instead of tender flakes of bream, straddling a too-small bicycle pointed down toward the scrap of sea. Tethys, who has never learned to swim.

"Don't go too far," she calls.

"To Vozrozhdeniya!"

"Don't you dare!" She'd never make it anyway. The island was 90 miles away.

They wait two days for police to drive up from Mo'ynoq. Normally, they would have buried Yusup immediately, but they were told to leave him until officers arrived. "They better not take too long, or he'll pickle in that salt," Marina says to her daughter.

"He was pickled already, Mama."

Besides Marina, Darya, Saiga and Tethys, there are a couple of Canadian schoolteachers from Tashkent, a British documentary filmmaker with her translator, Yusup's friend Arman, and the cook, Nuratdin.

"You can't see that part of the shore from the camp," Marina tells the detectives. "Anyone could have passed by." The men duck in and out of yurts, asking questions, walking with their chests out. One of them pats Tethys on the head and she flinches. Marina hates what the 11-year-old has already learned about men. She should never have left Darya here, never traveled so far. Or never come back.

She is in Mo'ynoq with her daughter's family when the officers knock again. "It's true he was drunk, but not so drunk it would kill him," they say. Marina wonders why they're even bothering to investigate. If anyone from outside cared whether they lived or died, they would still feel alive.

"So it was the glass?"

The taller officer looks at her for a long moment. "No," he says.

She looks at him back.

"Pristine," he finally says.

"Pristine?"

"The fungicide."

She sighs. "Oh, the fungicide. He used to sell it. So that makes sense."

"Not really. Not like this."

"What do you mean?"

"There's enough in his bloodstream to kill twenty men. You can't get that high a concentration just breathing it."

"Even for fifteen years?"

"Even for fifteen years. Was he still selling it?"

"He was too drunk to do much of anything anymore."

"He work with anyone?"

"Arman." They were partners, went farm to farm together in the truck, selling their clouds of poison.

"And this Arman is?"

"Two streets over," Darya says. "House with the green roof."

"Would he want to kill your husband, ma'am?"

Darya and Marina look at each other, carefully. They shrug.

"There's more," the man says. "He had certain other substances in his bloodstream."

"If it's anything agricultural and toxic, then we all do."

"More than that, I'm afraid. He had secret substances. Viruses. Things he should not have had access to."

"Like?"

"I'm not at liberty to say."

"But he's dead."

"It's not just about him. Can I ask, did he ever visit an island in the sea?"

Darya snorts. "An island? It's all island now. Used to be more than a thousand, but now we're just one big happy piece of dry land."

"A special island."

You mean the one that ate my husband? Marina does not say.

"Not that I know."

The officer closes his notebook, though he hasn't written a word.

"Call us if you think of anything."

"Of course."

"What was that about?" Marina asks when the men are gone. They're in the backyard, spreading corn for the chickens.

Darya doesn't have time to answer before Arman arrives with fresh condolences and a bottle. They sit outside while Tethys makes tea.

"I guess the business is yours now." Darya looks at him.

"Unless you want—"

"I want nothing of it."

He nods, pours the rest of his tea down his throat, stands.

"They weren't just selling Pristine."

Marina stares at her daughter.

"They also sold Venezuelan equine encephalitis. Anthrax. Tularemia."

"What—"

"They scraped them from the ruins on the island, sold them to the US. Black market. There is quite a lot of interest in what the Russians were up to on that island. That's how we paid for the truck, the bicycle." Darya waves her hand toward Tethys, pedaling circles in the street.

"You never—"

"You weren't here."

"Before or after Sergei? ..."

Darya looks down at her lap. "Before."

"And he died of—"

"Smallpox. They gave his body to the Americans. You wouldn't have wanted it back."

"No," says Marina.

The men return that night.

"Your friend Arman is dead."

"Friend—"

"We found this in his home." The officer lifts the sack of Pristine towards us.

"But he—"

"We found some in his teacup. Maybe he'd been drinking, thought it was sugar."

It didn't seem likely. Arman was too sharp, too predatory.

Marina wakes to the soft hand of her granddaughter on her cheek, the gleam of her eyes in the dark.

"I wanted them to stop killing the water."

"Tethys—"

"He wouldn't stop selling it so I put it in his bottle. And Arman's tea. In his house too, to be sure. Now there will be no more poisons."

"Oh, Tethys."

"Will the police come get me?"

"Listen to me, Tethys. Listen. You thought it was sugar, do you hear me? You thought it was sugar. It's a mistake anyone could make."

"Yes," her granddaughter echoes, "I thought it was sugar."

In the morning, Marina sweeps every grain from the house, buries it by the roots of the dead pear tree. She thinks how many poisons remain, how many cannot be washed away by the girl named for an ocean. When would they know, all the way through, that they and the earth were the same? That they are the sea. They were the sea.

After Arman is buried, the police drop the case. How can you find just one murderer in a town made of criminals?

A gentler knock interrupts lunch. Marina finds the filmmaker from the yurt camp and her translator. "You should have this," the filmmaker says. "I only just saw it two days ago in Nukus when I was editing."

Marina lets her in and makes tea. The filmmaker opens a tiny screen on her camera to play the footage, as Tethys climbs onto her lap.

It's filmed at night, with a long exposure.

There, tiny, is Yusup, his feet pinned by the sand, waving his bottle at the water. Then it comes over him, a wave that knocks him back and smashes his bottle against another. Trying to get up, he trips, the water pushes him forward, and he is impaled.

Tethys looks up at Marina. "I knew it wasn't sugar," she whispers in her ear. "But I guess the sea just wanted to be sure."

DON'T WANT TO KNOW

Steve Beresford

THE BEGINNING

"What are you up to?" Fran was trying not to get irritated. But she did get very irritated with Joey very quickly these days.

"Just looking for something," Joey said.

It was the way he said it, with too much innocence. Fran shivered with suspicion. She knew he was up to something. Again.

Joey, her husband, had come down and started rooting about in all the drawers and cupboards in the kitchen. She'd already heard him upstairs, moving about in the spare bedroom they used as a home office. He then moved on to the bedroom, opening and closing everything that could possibly be opened and closed.

"Looking for what?" Fran was getting dinner ready—it was her turn—and all the noise had set her nerves on edge. And now he was getting in the way. "That thing." Joey opened the drawer with the odds and ends in and rifled through the assorted contents.

"What thing?"

"You know, that thing. The whatsit. You use it for … Ah, here it is." He held up something that looked like a stunted misshapen screwdriver. Fran had no idea what it was and couldn't guess what its function might be. Much like a lot of stuff in that drawer. That was where Joey stashed items that he saved in case they one day turned out to be useful. Today was clearly that one day.

"Why were you looking for it upstairs first?"

"I wasn't. I was looking for something else then. I've been on a gathering mission."

"Right. And why do you want all these things you've gathered?"

Joey hesitated, giving Fran a strange look, as though considering what she would be happy with as a response. Then he said: "You don't want to know."

It chilled her blood, the way he said that.

"This is about Jamie, isn't it?"

Everything was about Jamie. Everything that went wrong was Jamie's fault. Everything that went right was one in the eye for Jamie. Hardly a day went by without Jamie's name being mentioned for one reason or another. Fran had taken about as much of it as she could and she was beginning to wish she didn't know either of them—not her husband nor his brother. This wasn't a marriage any more. Not really. Joey had become obsessed with getting back at Jamie to the exclusion of all else.

"Fran, honestly," Joey said, "you don't want to know."

She grabbed his arm, forcing him to face her. "No, go on, tell me. I do want to know."

Joey smiled. "I'm going to kill Jamie." Like saying it relieved the pressure inside him.

THE HISTORY

Joey and Jamie hated each other.

And they hated each other because of Fran.

Joey and Jamie Carran were brothers. Joey was two years younger than Jamie. They were similar in so many ways, almost like twins, and yet so different too. Fran met Jamie first. He was handsome, fun and intelligent. One date led to another, and another, and several more. But six weeks later, although Fran was enjoying herself, she didn't really feel the spark that keeps two people together. She knew it wasn't going anywhere.

Then she met Joey. He returned from some month-long business trip abroad and stepped into her life by accident when she met Jamie by surprise at his office.

Joey was also handsome, fun and intelligent. But more so, somehow. The spark was there immediately. Joey felt it too. It was a tricky thing, exchanging one brother for the other, but she did it as gently and as kindly as she good. And for a while, right up until the wedding 18 months later in fact, Fran thought Jamie was cool with their relationship. Though she did realise, when she looked back later, after Jamie's meltdown, that the signs were there he was simmering unhappily.

Then, at the reception, an argument started between Joey and Jamie. Jamie called Fran some terrible names. He accused Joey of stealing her from him. He said that he couldn't ever forgive either of them for what they had done to him.

Deep and long-repressed rage exploded out of him with such vehemence and bitterness.

"I loved you," Jamie screamed. "And you betrayed me. You both betrayed me. I hate you. I wish you were dead!"

What made it worse was that the brothers ran a company together. Software engineering, started from scratch and built into a successful, thriving business. That's where Joey was, when Fran first started dating Jamie: trying to build up an overseas client base.

And the company offices were completely open plan, with the brothers' desks facing each other. The open wound in Jamie's mind had obviously festered with every day he spent sitting just a couple of metres away from Joey, listening to his calls to Fran, watching them laugh and kiss and cuddle at the opposite desk. Not that the desks stayed that way for long after Jamie's outburst at the wedding. When Joey returned from his and Fran's honeymoon he found his desk in a corner, facing a blank wall.

It was inevitable really, afterwards, that more bad things would begin to happen.

THE PLAN

"I'm going to kill Jamie." Joey stood in the kitchen. He was calm, his tone relaxed, like he was talking about popping down the corner shop for a jar of coffee.

Fran even laughed, "Yeah, right," initially thinking it was simply a joke, something to say so that when he told her the real reason he was foraging about it wouldn't sound so awful in comparison.

"No, seriously," Joey said. "I have this plan. It's brilliant."

"What are you talking about? When you say kill, you mean ..."

"I mean: I'm going to kill Jamie."

"You can't!"

"Why not?"

"Because ..." Fran had grown to really dislike Jamie after all that had happened, but killing him was a little extreme. "It's wrong, for a start. Plus, you'd get caught and go to prison—and how would that help anyone?"

"Ah, well now," Joey said, "that's the beautiful part, you see. It's not going to look like murder. It's going to look like a tragic but perfectly innocent accident. I have it all worked out. Every last detail."

"You're crazy."

"I've been crazy for the past two years."

Two years was the length of their marriage. Well, thanks very much, Fran thought.

"Now I'm feeling sane again," Joey said.

"It's ridiculous. You can't go around killing people. Especially your own brother."

"He's not my brother. Not any more. He stopped being my brother at our wedding. Doubly so when he cheated me out of the company. I want what's rightfully mine and this is the only way."

Joey had never come to terms with being chucked out of the company. Within weeks of their return from the honeymoon—and what a fun occasion that had been, with Joey still seething after all the hoo-ha at the wedding—Jamie had cooked up a clever scheme to legally dissolve their partnership while retaining complete control of the business.

"If Jamie's dead," Joey said, "then I have a chance of taking back the company. It should be mine anyway. It was my idea."

It was a familiar refrain: it's mine; he cheated me; I hate him. Fran had heard it all before. And she often encouraged Joey with his attempts to legally regain what he once possessed. But she only had a finite supply of patience and encouragement, which was dwindling fast. Mostly, these days, she simply wanted to forget Jamie even existed and move on so she and Joey could have a happy life together, not one tainted by Jamie's hatred of them.

"So when," Fran asked, "are you thinking of doing it?" Crikey, what a question! But Fran could see the determination on Joey's face and she had to know what sort of timescale she had to talk her husband down from this awful precipice on which he was teetering.

"Thursday," Joey said.

"Thursday?" Today was Sunday.

"I'd do it sooner, but there's a lot to get in place first. You see, I'm going to …"

She held up a hand, cutting him off. "No, don't tell me."

"But it's a fantastic plan."

"I don't care."

"It all relies on …"

"No, you were right." Fran pushed past him, dinner forgotten, desperate only to be as far away as possible from the nightmare the two brothers had plunged her into. "I don't want to know."

THE DEVICE

Joey spent the rest of Sunday in the shed. Fran watched for a time from the bedroom window. She could hear hammering and drilling, but when Joey finally emerged after it had gone dark he wasn't carrying anything. And he slept in the spare room.

She did try talking to him the next morning, but he was in too much of a rush.

"I have errands to run," he said. "We'll talk when I get back."

"Where are you going?"

"Here and there. Remember ..." And his voice was so cold. "... you don't want to know." Then he was gone.

Fran called in sick to work—she was a librarian at the university—because she simply couldn't face it. This murder plan of Joey's had thrown her into turmoil. Joey was obviously serious. Deadly serious. She knew she had to do something, but she couldn't decide what.

She could start though, she reckoned, by seeing what was in the shed.

A device stood on the workbench. It was about 18 inches square and had a winding mechanism and a flywheel. She couldn't fathom what it did. She went to touch it, but stopped herself, snatching her hand away.

Fingerprints.

If this was part of Joey's grand plan to murder his brother then she didn't want to involve herself in it by inadvertently leaving behind any evidential trace on his equipment.

Quite how this could be used to kill someone and make it look like an accident was beyond her. But really she didn't want to know. The how was far less important than the when.

She called her friend, Abi. "You free? I need to have a chat."

"About what?" Abi wanted to know.

"Well, it's sort of complicated ..."

THE FRIEND

"Murder?" Abi was frowning.

Fran nodded. They were in the café of the garden centre at Tatenhill, tucked away on a corner table.

"If, hypothetically speaking," Fran said, "you knew someone was planning to commit murder ..."

"Actual murder?" Abi couldn't seem to take in what Fran was saying to her, couldn't seem to process the crucial word.

"Yes, actual murder, as in killing someone." Fran tried to frame it as an abstract concept, not blurt out that Joey was in the middle of planning it. "If you knew about it beforehand, theoretically, what would you do?"

"Is this like one of those questionnaires you get in magazines?" Abi did love those pick-A-B-or-C things in the glossies. "Depending on what I answer, you tell me whether I'm a psychopath or not?"

"Something like that, yes. In fact, yes, it's exactly that. Although not a magazine, but it is a test I read about online."

"Go on, then. Ask me."

"So, what would you do? If you knew?"

Abi raised her eyebrows. "About? ..."

Fran suppressed the urge to sigh, beginning to wish she had called a more sensible best friend, a friend who was not quite so ditzy and excitable and hard to explain things to. "If you knew someone, hypothetically, was about to commit murder and ..."

"Right! Yes! I see! Oh well ..." Abi gave it a lot of thought. "What's the point of the murder?"

"What?"

"I mean, is this hypothetical person murdering for money? For love? For ... For revenge?"

"Let's say revenge."

Abi leant forward. "Ooh, interesting! Who am I getting revenge on? And why?"

"Does it matter?"

"It's the difference, isn't it, between victims and how much they deserve it. Someone from college who bullied you years ago is completely different to someone who, for example, stole your life savings or killed your dog." It sounded like Abi had been contemplating revenge for some time, and in great detail. "It's a different mindset altogether."

"I suppose it is. Okay, assume it's for money then, if it's simpler." Maybe revenge as a motive was a little too close to home anyway for a hypothetical chat. "You want to murder someone to make a profit."

"How much profit?"

"I don't know." Crikey! "A lot."

"How much is a lot? If we're talking a few thousand, enough for a holiday, murder's a bit extreme. But if we're talking, like, millions, then that might be worth it."

"Call it a life-changing amount of money."

"Fine. And how urgently do I need this money?"

"What?"

"Because that makes a difference too. It's like with revenge. Revenge, you can usually take your time, unless there's some artificial deadline, like someone leaving the country or changing their will or something. But under normal circumstances I'd imagine you can often plan and pick your moment."

Normal circumstances? When would it ever be normal to murder someone?

"But money!" Abi continued. "I'd guess it's a more immediate thing. More desperate. You could be in a real hole, needing instant cash and oodles of it so that the loan shark doesn't ..."

"Abi!" This had become ridiculous. Fran got the feeling she could be here all day, going through every single permutation of murder, before she got any help from her friend. "Never mind. Okay? Just forget it."

"No, no, come on. I'm enjoying this. I want to find out if I'm a psychopath or not."

"I think that's already obvious." Who else put this much thought into hypothetical murder—apart from an actual murderer?

Abi sat back. "There's no need to take that tone."

"Sorry." Fran wanted advice. And she knew she was probably asking the wrong person. But who else could help her?

Abi, however, leant forward again, dropping her voice. "Are you in trouble?"

"Me?" Fran shook her head. "No!"

"Are you?" Suddenly her real friend appeared, not the ditzy one, but the one who was always there when Fran needed her. "Is that what this is about?"

"Of course not!"

"Fran ..."

Fran cracked. "Okay, yes." Her eyes abruptly filled with tears. "I'm in trouble."

"What sort of trouble?"

And Fran couldn't help herself. "You don't want to know."

THE THREAT

"I thought you'd be at work," Joey said, when Fran returned home from the garden centre café.

"Couldn't face it. Not with you and ... and your ..." She'd driven up to find him unloading the boot of his car. He had a strimmer, a length of chain, a table lamp and other stuff. "What's all that for?"

"Wouldn't like to say." He took out a plastic crate and carried it down the side entry, then to the shed. Fran followed. "Anyway, if you haven't been to work," he unlocked the padlock, "where have you been?"

"Chatting with Abi."

He took the crate inside and Fran watched as he unloaded it—various bit and pieces, screws, washers, hooks, hinges—on to the workbench.

"Chatting about what?"

"This and that."

"Fran ..." His voice became threatening.

"I wanted some advice."

"About me and my plan? And you went to Abi?" He laughed briefly. "I bet that went well."

"I'm scared, Joey. I don't want you doing this. It's not right."

"The brilliant thing about my plan, Fran, is that it really is foolproof. Even if you go to the police there'll be no evidence to link me to Jamie's death. Honestly, I've thought of everything. In fact, it's all I've thought about for the past few months. The police won't bother investigating because they won't even suspect a crime has taken place. But, just to make sure you do keep quiet—I have my reputation to think of, after all—I can build in a failsafe mechanism. One tiny change and it's you who'll get the blame. I'll say it was some sort of love triangle thing and that you wanted to permanently shut Jamie up. I'll get everything I want, but you'll be the one who ends up in prison."

"Are you threatening me?" She went cold to the core. She was seeing a side to Joey that he had managed to keep hidden since she'd met him.

"Cross me, Fran, and suffer the consequences." He stepped in close, so close she could smell his vengeful rage. "I want my company back. Nothing, not even you, is going to stop me."

THE REALISATION

Up until that point, Fran half-believed it was a joke. Half-believed that Joey would see a fatal flaw in his plan. Half-believed that he simply wouldn't have the courage to carry it through. Half-believed, too, that she could do something to stop him.

But she could see now that so many halves didn't add up properly to a whole.

She realised her part in this mad scheme was, for Joey, almost non-existent. He wasn't doing this for her or because of her. What Jamie had said and done with regard to her meant nothing. All the lies Jamie had spread and the rumours he'd started—

they were basically background noise. To Joey, only the company and getting it back mattered.

Turned out, she realised, she hadn't picked the better brother after all. Neither one was better than the other.

Life with Joey had been wonderful. To start with. But it wasn't long before the cracks began to show. The open wound that was the rift between Joey and Jamie had become so seriously infected that it was contaminating everything around it too.

Fran suddenly realised that being married to her, for Joey, was incidental, possibly even an inconvenience.

She also realised that on Thursday Jamie could die—in fact, most likely would die—and Joey would be responsible.

She had to do something.

But what?

THE PHONE CALL

Fran dithered.

She wondered whether to make a call to the police. In her desperation, she almost called Abi again. She very nearly called Jamie himself.

Monday became Tuesday, then Wednesday.

Fran started to panic. What if she was too late? What if Joey's plan was already in motion and impossible to stop until its unalterable conclusion?

No!

She couldn't let it happen.

She couldn't.

So she made a call.

THE POLICE

Joey went out early on Thursday. Fran pleaded with him, but he ignored her, roughly shaking her off as she grasped his arm and physically tried to hold him back.

"Joey! No!"

"You can't stop me!"

"Please, Joey!"

"I thought you'd be glad. This will put an end to all my misery and give me back the life I should have."

Fran still had no idea where Joey was going or what he was going to do. At first she didn't want to know. Then he wouldn't tell her. Now …

Now, the emptiness inside, the lack of any concrete knowledge about the plan, was unbearable. She only hoped that her telephone call had made some difference.

The police arrived on Thursday evening. It was odd that Joey hadn't returned by then, but maybe that was part of his plan too. Or maybe he was simply never returning to her now he was getting what he wanted.

"Mrs Carran?"

"It's about Jamie, isn't it?"

"Jamie Carran?" The policeman was momentarily confused. "Yes, madam, I suppose it is."

"Is he? …"

"Yes, madam. Jamie Carran is under arrest. In connection with the suspicious death of your husband."

And it took a few moments for that to register. "What?"

Joey was dead? No, surely they had it the wrong way round.

"I'm very sorry, madam. Perhaps we should continue this inside."

THE END

Fran didn't know the details. The police were reluctant to say much at all, apart from the basic facts—which were that Joey was dead and Jamie had been arrested.

Jamie asked to see her from his holding cell at the police station and Fran now sat in an interview room with her brother-in-law.

"If you hadn't called me," Jamie said, "I'd be dead now."

Yes, Fran decided in the end to call Jamie, not the police. As it was she had to leave a message on his voicemail. He never did actually take a call from her. She was surprised her number wasn't blocked on his phone, surprised he'd even listened to her message, rather than simply deleting it.

But what was most surprising was this outcome.

"I was rather hoping to stop both of you getting hurt," she said. She felt hollow. Empty. Adrift. Joey, the husband she once loved, was gone. Dead. And yet the pain of that loss simply wasn't there.

"Joey's plan would have been perfect," Jamie said, "if you hadn't warned me he was coming. But the way it panned out, it was either him or me." He smiled thinly. "And now he's gone. And I can claim it was self-defence." He didn't seem bothered that his own brother was now dead. "I have to admire the sheer audacity of his design though." His gaze wandered wistfully. "Wish I'd thought of it myself actually." If anything, he seemed jealous, as he had been from the start, as though Joey was still getting one over him, even from the other side.

The two brothers were more alike than they would ever admit—always more concerned with themselves than anybody else. Fran now wondered whether either had really loved her, or whether she had simply been an unwitting pawn in their power game.

"I suppose," Jamie said, "you know about his plan. About his clever machine. About everything he organised to bring an end to my life."

Fran shook her head. "I haven't the foggiest actually."

"You haven't? Didn't you help him plan it?"

"I had nothing to do with it. I only ever tried to stop him."

"But he told you all about it, surely?"

"Not a word." Fran saw the possible components in the shed before they were assembled—the device, the strimmer, the lamp and all that—but had no idea how Joey was going to use them to commit the perfect murder and walk away with no suspicion attached to him.

Jamie laughed. "Shall I tell you what he was planning then? Shall I tell you how I turned his own plan against him?"

Fran thought about it. A part of her was curious, but it was a very tiny part. "No thanks."

"No point keeping it secret," Joey said. "The police know everything anyway. And I'll probably get off. Self-defence, you see. Which is one in the eye for Joey." Jamie laughed again. "Or it would be … if he were still here."

"It's still no."

"You don't want to know?" He was surprised.

Fran stood up. She didn't want to be here and she had already heard more than enough. She wished she'd never met either brother. They'd brought her nothing but pain and sorrow. And some things—including the plan for a perfect murder—were simply better not to know.

It was time to walk away and start a new life without either of them.

"Actually," she said, "I absolutely don't want to know."

THE ELEVATING POWER OF ART

Liv Strom

Jane and Ricky were drinking at O'Malley's, as was their usual in-between work routine, though this time the mood was as low as their funds. Their last job had ended badly, but who could have planned on a runaway elephant? Sure, they were robbing a circus, but that was just not a thing an average thief could be expected to handle during a heist. Mitigating circumstances, they called it, but that didn't help them pay for the third round of drinks, or their debts to people even more unsavoury than themselves. It did, however, put them in an accepting mood when a lanky, dark, fix-foot fellow in a jacket better suited to a lecture hall, and a nose large enough to give elephant flashbacks offered to pay.

He introduced himself as John, the made-up name an apt show of his lack of imagination. When the third round was drunk, he cut to the chase.

"I sometimes work with the Royal Museum of Art. When someone gets ill, or they are busy, they call me in. I'm an art historian and painter, you see."

Ricky grunted noncommittally. He'd never seen much art, but held out hope that the stranger might spring for a fourth round if he nodded in the right place.

"A week ago they called me to support writing the Certificates of Authenticity for the donations from Belcherly Manor. You've heard about Belcherly, right?"

"That's the one where the old guy croaked and left it all to charity despite the grandson screaming that it's his?" Ricky said, feeling proud of reading the newspaper once in a blue moon.

Jane, who in her white shirt and jeans resembled a female James Dean, was not as patient. "As fascinating as this is, we have places to be, people to see."

John waved his arms as if hunting an acrobatic fly to get her to remain in her seat. "I want to hire you. For an ... acquisition."

She raised an eyebrow. People often thought Ricky, the six-foot-plus giant, was the more dangerous one. They hadn't seen Jane angry, and something about John was like a rat gnawing at her already frayed nerves.

"As I mentioned, I'm an accomplished painter and after inspecting the art I produced replicas of the three most valuable ones. They're already packaged for shipping to the Museum, no one will check them again. I need your help to switch them out. I'll pay you 50k." John dabbed his perspiring forehead.

Ricky leaned forward, lowering his voice. "You want our help in switching out three paintings tomorrow night?"

"Too short notice," Jane replied, ignoring Ricky.

"But we'll be *art thieves*," Ricky said, imagining dashing gentlemen thieves with sophisticated moustaches and admiring fans. That would be an upgrade from snatching circus funds and prize-winning dogs. And there definitely wouldn't be any elephants.

John's eyes wandered between the pair. "It'll be empty and I even know the security code."

Ricky and Jane gave each other the kind of long look which they had perfected while working together for thirteen years. Jane broke first and turned to John. "Order another round and tell us all you know about the place."

After the sixth pint, they had both a plan and an agreement.

Unfortunately, it was *not* a dark and stormy night. Instead, the full moon shone like a headlight, illuminating what was best described as a gothic stone castle surrounded by manicured hedges and scantily clad female statues. *Damned bad night for a burglary*, Ricky thought as they stepped out of the unmarked white van they secured for the evening. Neither Ricky nor Jane had a car of their own; what was the point when others left theirs standing around? And John, nervously sweating despite only arriving at the scene, didn't seem to want Jane or Ricky within reach of his private property.

The three of them wore less easily obtained uniforms from Security Now. Finding the laundry company and snatching the uniforms had been enough for Jane to question the job again, but Ricky was set. Their reputation needed this. He already saw himself drinking expensive wine in a black turtleneck.

When the real security guard rounded a corner, Jane hefted a tool as multifunctional as a Swiss army knife—her crowbar. Ricky blocked her. When a mountain shaped like a refrigerator interferes, you either stop or break your nose. Jane stopped.

"We're being *art thieves*, Janey. Art thieves don't smash people over the head, they trick and beguile."

Jane craned her neck to meet Ricky's eyes. "Beguile? With what?"

But he was already approaching the guard. In resignation, Jane slipped further into the dark, pulling a stumbling John along with her, while cursing art and amateurs.

"Company sent me to take over," Ricky said, stepping into the flashlight beam.

The guard frowned. "I've got another two hours. No way they're cutting my shift short." The guy looked ready to fight over it.

"They said something about your wife calling. Or maybe mother," Ricky said, putting on a smile meant to calm, but it had gotten so used to threatening that it no longer knew how to do anything else.

The guard stepped away from the giant confronting him and reached for the cell on his belt. "Just wait a second." He took another step backwards, and a dull thud sounded through the calm night. Glazed eyes tried to focus on Ricky, mouth still moving, before collapsing like he'd been hit by a car rather than Jane's crowbar. She called that excellent technique.

She wiped the blood off before slipping the crowbar back into her go bag. "You're right, a bit of beguiling, and he never saw it coming."

"Jane! I had him," Ricky said, throwing the limp body over his shoulder, and deciding that he at least, had behaved like a gentleman.

First it all went smashingly well. John's codes worked and in less than half an hour they had stuffed the guard in the wine cellar, jammed the door shut with an antique chair, found the art and carefully broken open the packing crates John indicated.

While John was busy taking out and wrapping up the real paintings, Ricky got his first look at the fakes. Surrealist landscapes made him wonder what drugs painters back in the day took, and where he could procure some. He looked closer with the flashlight, a frown appearing between his bushy eyebrows. He called Jane over. She pulled up the image of the original on her phone. Even in the miniature picture on the screen, they could see that the horse was supposed to be white. And a horse.

"John, come over here." Jane's voice was colder than a mule in Moscow.

Having got the last of the originals into the art carriers, John stepped up. If he'd had a survival instinct, he would have been walking in the other direction. Instead he whispered, "*Hurry.*"

"Hurry with what? Didn't you say that you authenticate art? This is *not* the same picture."

He frowned, looking at his own painting. "Maybe the light at home …"

Ricky felt his dream of a new level of thievery evaporate. "It's a donkey."

Sweat dripped from John's neck and he tried to loosen the security uniform's collar. He pulled out a pen. "Maybe if I add a saddle."

Ricky kept Jane from strangling John, reminding her that they would be paid either way and with an hour left until the next security guard was to turn up, they had stuffed the ruined fakes into the crates, hoping that they might at least delay the pursuit.

Ricky looked morosely at the twenty-two remaining art crates, but a missing crate would be noticed before they were even loaded for transport. Then John let out the kind of scream that perforated eardrums and in Jane's mind shouldn't exist outside cheap horror flicks.

She slammed her hand over his mouth and followed his eyes. On the other side of the window a young man, as tall as Ricky but built like a flagpole and not out of the pimply awkward stage everyone suppressed as soon as they could, was wiping down the glass and wooden frames. Letting go of John, Jane jerked up the antique window and hauled the boy inside. He landed on his ass and Ricky aimed his flashlight in the already wide eyes.

"I'm just washing the windows, okay? For the sale tomorrow, I was late and—"

Jane, who had a hard time remembering that she was an art thief, slapped him. "It's night. No one washes windows at night."

The bucket which the boy had been holding had followed him into the room and water now spread across the floor. Ricky bent down to sniff it and smiled. "That ain't no water. Lighter fluid, if you ask me." And Ricky knew lighter fluid, burning things, having been a gateway crime for a five-year-old left alone at home once too often.

John jumped out of the liquid, attempting to wipe his feet on the antique oriental carpet. Ricky winced at the waste, while Jane focused on the young man at her feet. A lightbulb flickered to life in the back of her mind. "You have one chance, boy. Truth this time, or we will haul you to the police ourselves." Talking to the police was the oldest threat in the book. No one suspected wrongdoing if *you* called the cops.

"Okay, okay. No one was supposed to be in here. I didn't know they upped the security." Jane frowned, and the boy sped up. "I'm Archibald Belcherly. All this belongs to me."

The lightbulb was no longer flickering. "I thought there were no heirs."

"None he approved of, the bastard."

Ricky, never far behind Jane, reached down to help the boy up. "And you thought burning it down would show the old man? We get it. He might be dead, but you never know if he is still watching."

Archibald, now on his feet, shrugged. "Well, yeah. He changed the door code and the window frames are the only flammable thing I could get to. I've finally washed every single one. Could we, you know, forget about this?"

John, still on the oriental carpet, found the backbone he had previously misplaced. "Certainly not. You planned to burn *art*. To deprive anyone from experiencing the beauty your family collected over the centuries because you hated your grandfather? Prison is too good."

Jane and Ricky's shared smile grew. Ricky pulled a hand through his hair. "John has a point, Archie. I understand, I do. If my family wrote me out of their wills, I would make them pay. But we're hired to move and guard these paintings. Would lose our jobs if something happened to them." He shook his head.

Archibald licked his lips. "You're moving the art to the museum? I thought you were coming tomorrow."

"Yeah, safer to transport at night. Art thieves, you know," Jane said and looked at her watch. Thirty-two minutes until shift change. "We're just about to start loading."

John opened his mouth, but whatever he meant to say came out as yelp when Ricky stepped on his toes. Amateurs never saw the larger picture. You had to help them along.

"What if I help you load, and then after you leave, I, you know?" Archibald even wiggled his eyebrows suggestively. Jane wondered if she had ever been that young, then remembered the blood red motorcycle she snatched at fourteen because her sister bet her she couldn't jump Mission Canyon. She had won the bed, but killed the bike. It made her feel something close to affection for the kid. It's not everyday you could help a criminal virgin cross the line.

She bit her lip. "Well, the next shift starts in twenty-eight minutes." The boy hefted the first crate and was on his way out the door before Jane finished speaking.

With seven minutes to spare, only the fakes remained inside. Sweat dripped from their noses and the van was packed tight enough to make any legitimate art transporter cry. Ricky was back to dreaming about wine and turtlenecks, but seeing the load before him, his imagination now placed him in Paris. Perhaps in a café with a large chested woman across his lap speaking passionately in French, Ricky not understanding a word in no way limiting the experience.

Jane pulled out her go-bag, which had saved her from situations ranging from prison to blind dates. Disregarding the rope, nail gun, inflatable life vest and thimble, she retrieved the flame thrower, handing it to the kid together with her second-best smile.

"This, Archie, is a job for something larger than a box of matches. You've five minutes. Make Grandpa turn over in his grave. Maybe you'll even see the insurance money, lots of law firms who might take the case if there is no art left for the Museum to claim." She followed it with a business card containing only a phone number. "Return it when you're done, it's an heirloom."

With a cheerful wave, she joined the others in the van. Archie turned on the flamethrower, excitement shining in his eyes, and the nearest window lit like a bonfire.

Ricky drove the thieves along the dark road with headlights off, pulling over into the dark before the first turn. A security car sped past them towards Belcherly as flames painted the night sky red.

"I feel like we've forgotten something," Jane said at the same time as Ricky exclaimed: "The security guard!"

They stared at each other, and the silent argument went something like this:

Drive, Ricky, we have the load of a lifetime.

But the guard, Janey.

This is the lucky break we've been waiting for.

Art thieves don't hurt anyone. We don't hurt anyone.

Damn.

By now Ricky was already racing back up the road.

"What are you doing? We're going the wrong way!" John, who'd been left out of the silent argument, exclaimed.

Jane turned to answer as Ricky crashed into a manicured hedge and killed the motor. "We're robbers, possibly *art thieves*, not murderers. Stay put, guard the car and we'll be back soon. Do nothing and they won't see you." Jane, who gave it a snowball's chance in hell that John and the art would be there when they returned, grabbed her go bag.

With that, Jane and Ricky ran towards what resembled Thornfield Hall after the wife got loose. Archie had done well. The newly arrived security guard who had sped past them on the road stood screaming into a phone. Sirens sounded in the distance and, wishing they were closer, Jane suffered sudden vertigo, and knew for her doing the right thing was definitely wrong.

They faced each other one last time before entering the building. After too many mad dashes no last words were needed, they had taken care of those in 1998.

As luck had it, most of the building was stone, and the way down to the basement was next to the entrance. With only mild smoke inhalation and serious sweating, they arrived at the blocked door.

Jane removed the chair and Ricky rushed inside. Now, they knew why they were there, but they also knew there was a fair chance this heist wouldn't help settle their debts, so they made the best out of the situation while picking up the unconscious security guard.

Stumbling up the stairs and outside while coughing up their lungs, Ricky struggled with the guard and Jane gripped her go bag with both hands, swearing when it hit the stairs.

Seeing the lack of a white van and the three squad cars pull up to the house, they froze. For Ricky, who was lugging along the security guard, this topped the elephant. Jane dropped the bag as her hands rose above her head without waiting for instructions from her brain. Then a cheer went up, and the firefighters started spraying a house anyone with eyes knew was a lost cause. Jane lowered her arms and desperately tried to remember what innocence looked like. She was saved by the paramedics arriving. Handing over the unconscious guard, Jane and Ricky and the bag were taken to the ambulance. The nurse insisted they ride along to the hospital, and thus they had a first-rate view of passing the unmarked white van on the roadside, John pressed against the hood and the police officer opening the trunk.

Before dawn they were back at O'Malley's, following it all on the grimy TV over the bar. The surviving donkey painting and John's face were on every channel. This time they had brought their own wine. One of the five bottles of 1774 Vercel *Vin Jaune d'Arbois,* last sold at auction for $120k, Jane had added to the go bag. The first toast was dedicated to French wine, their two-hundred-fifty minutes as art thieves, and Archibald Belcherly, who by the third glass called to thank them. And ask Jane on a date, but that's another story.

HAPPY TO HELP

Carl Robinette

There's something my dad always says—If everyone cared more about being helpful and less about being happy, we'd all be a lot happier. But I guess some people think they can be the happiest on Earth and they make themselves miserable trying get there. Or maybe a person's levels of happiness and helpfulness come down to brain chemistry—it doesn't really matter. I'm just saying it's good to be helpful. And that's exactly what I was trying to do.

I had just left from visiting my dad on his houseboat. I was walking out to my car when I saw one of Dad's neighbors who I knew. He was standing next to a giant olive-green car, some vinyl top land yacht from fifty years ago.

Ray Gage was jiggling the door handle and saying something like, "I mean it. I'll wait until you run out of air, kid. I don't care."

There was a towheaded little kid inside the car with a gappy grin and a thousand-yard stare. I said hi to Gage.

"Huh?," he said. "Oh hey, Daisy."

I asked him what was up.

Gage told me the "little jackelope" had locked himself in the car with the keys.

I said, "This is your car?" and laughed.

Gage told me to get bent, the car was a classic. Then he flipped the kid his middle finger through the car window. The kid laughed. It was just another gorgeous quiet day down by the marina. Squalling seagulls, whispering palms, wispy clouds, the whole deal.

"Who is that kid anyway?" I asked Gage.

The kid was licking the window and giving us the stank eye.

Gage said, "My lady friend's son."

"Lady friend?" I said.

He shrugged and goes, "I'm going to kill this kid."

I told him how the kid probably just wanted attention and to let me see if I could talk to him. Kids are always more comfortable with women anyway. Ray said the kid's name was Carter. I hunched down and looked at him through the glass.

I told the kid something like, "Hi Carter. What's up, we're just hanging out, ok? No big deal. Just two cool buds and stuff. Nobody's mad at you. So what do you say you come out of there and we'll all go get some ice cream together?"

After a short staring contest, the kid opened the door a crack. He waved me closer like he wanted to whisper a secret. But when I got down eye-to-eye with him, the little hell-spawn spit in my face. Then he told me to eat shit, slammed the door shut and locked it again.

Gage handed me a clean hanky. Ray Gage was a back-pocket-hanky kind of guy. I wiped my face and tried handing the used cloth back to him and he told me to trash it.

I said, "That little kid is a huge asshole."

"Yup," Gage nodded.

I wanted to know if Gage thought I'd catch a disease from the kid's spit.

He said, "Probably. I'm surprised that loogie wasn't made of sulfuric acid. Burn right through your skull."

I wanted to know how Gage got stuck watching the kid.

He said, "I don't know. Manipulation. I think his mom might be smarter than me."

The kid was honking the horn now, just laying on it and cackling at us.

I used to carry brass knuckles in my purse before some off-duty cops confiscated them at some crappy concert I went to. They said they could've arrested me for carrying them. After that I started carrying one of those collapsible batons instead. I call it my whip bat and I whipped it out right then and there, took two strides and smashed out the back driver's side window of Ray's car. Then I unlocked the doors and hauled the little kid out. I stood him up and stuffed the phlegm-soaked hanky into the tiny pocket of his pants.

I pointed the whip bat at the kid and said, "I'm getting ice cream without you now."

Gage was pissed about his window. He goes, "What the hell?"

I told him his lady friend should pay for it. It was her kid's fault anyway. I saved the kid. He could have suffocated.

All Gage said was, "My window, Daisy."

I figured, you can't argue with results. After all, Gage did get his keys back.

He didn't see my point.

I helped him sweep up the glass and tape up the window with a garbage bag.

I gave Gage some money. He said it wasn't enough to cover the repair. It probably wasn't, but it was all the cash I had on me. So then I said something really stupid.

I said, "Sorry. I owe you, OK."

I had a low-grade sweet tooth building and a rumble in my stomach, but I wasn't really in the mood for ice cream, so I cruised up the block to Steve's Rinky Dink Coffee. I ordered two quesadillas Salvadoreñas and a humungous caramelized whipped something-or-other with extra whip and an extra shot of espresso. When I turned around form the counter I bumped into a man standing behind me.

The man was built like a fireplug. He gnashed his jaws at me, a mean glean in his eye. It was Thomas Dooley.

He said, "You again."

Dooley was a local comic shop owner and half-assed criminal entrepreneur who was known to deal in stolen collectibles. I'd had a violent run-in with him about a year earlier.

Dooley goes, "You're that brat who smashed my face with brass knuckles last year."

Then he got all pouty and told some sob story about having to have his jaw wired shut or something.

My mouth was full of pastry when I said, "Oh um, well yeah, you kinda pulled a gun on me. What did you think would happen?"

Dooley said something like, "Ew. God, do you always talk with your mouth full? What is that you're eating anyway?"

"Quesadilla," I told him.

Dooley said it didn't look like any quesadilla he ever saw. I told him it was a Salvadorian quesadilla. It was some kind of crumbly cornbread cream cheese and sesame deliciousness.

I said, "I don't really know what's in it but I think there's about a stick of butter in every bite. It's amazing. Try some."

I proffered my second unwrapped pastry and he slapped it out of my hand to the ground.

"What the hell man. That was a peace offering," I told him.

Dooley said he was leaving. He didn't like the class of clientele at Steve's Rinky Dink anymore.

Some people.

I picked up the quesadilla in its cellophane package and was on my way. So far it was looking like a pretty crappy day and all the gorgeous weather in the world wasn't going to de-crap it. I sat in my car, parked in a loading zone out front and ate.

Just as I was eating the last crumb off of my shirt front, there was the wail of police sirens and about fifty black-and-white SUVs flew by with their lights flashing, reckless speed on the narrow beachfront street. In my mirror, I watched them hook a left into the West Harbor Marina where I'd just been visiting with my dad. I started the car and did an eleven-point turn on the narrow street.

Back in the marina parking lot, I can't honestly say I was surprised to find they were arresting Ray Gage. Of course he was my friend, but Gage was a grade-A dirt bag. Although, I kind of always saw him as a stand-up guy, in his own way. I mean, you couldn't trust Ray Gage not to steal from you, but you could trust him to pay you back whenever he did rip you off. But I guess what floored me that day was the reason for his arrest. They were taking Ray Gage down for the Big H—Homicide.

There was a small crowd watching the police put Gage in the back of a car. Hands cuffed behind his back and everything. I found my dad and he filled me in—a woman stabbed to death on Gage's boat. Dad said the marina's rent-a-cop caught Gage in there, literally red-handed. The victim's kid was there too and the "poor little guy" saw the whole thing. Carter, the poor little reptilian hell beast.

I wasn't ready to believe Gage had killed his lady friend. I told this to my dad and he told me how Gage had a pretty "seamy" past and wasn't the "friendly neighborhood slacker" I thought he was.

I said, "Yeah, but you don't really think he murdered someone do you?"

"I don't know, Poopernickle," he told me. "But do us all a favor and keep your nose out of it for once."

I saw the marina's rent-a-cop lingering in the crowd and I told Dad I'd see him later.

I think my dad said, "Poopernickle" to my back but I was already long gone.

The rent-a-cop was a twenty-something woman I knew from high school. Her name was Rita. She looked like a meter maid in her security company costume.

She said, "Daisy. Hey."

I asked her what had happened.

"Dude," Rita told me. "It was crazy, and super-super gross, but mostly crazy."

Apparently Rita had heard a woman scream—a bad scream. She thought it had come from Gage's boat, the Dawn Star. Rita said she only boarded the boat purely because she felt she had to check on the scream, ethically. In the boat's cabin she found Gage standing over the woman's body, blood on his hands and the kid crying and hiding down in a corner of the boat.

"I don't really know anything else," Rita said.

"Who was the woman," I asked.

"She's Louise Schaffer," Rita said. "I guess her dad invented online dating or something."

"Schaffer? Like Schaffer, Schaffer?" I asked her.

Rita said that was the Schaffer she meant alright, these were some serious Silicon Valley dynasty folks.

"Louise Schaffer," I said. "It's so sad."

"Whatever," Rita said.

"Wasn't she married," I asked.

Rita told me that Louise Schaffer had been a divorcee. Her ex-husband was some musician guy from one of those 1990s swing revival groups that had been almost-famous.

"No crap?" I said. "I've heard of that band."

"Yeah," Rita said.

I told her my money was on the husband killing the woman. Rita wanted to know why I would think that. She said she had found Ray Gage in there right after the woman screamed.

"Yeah, but it's always the husband," I shrugged.

That night I was drinking at some divey jazz hall up on the Mesa in the north part of town. It was my first time in a jazz bar and I guess I had imagined they would brazenly flout anti-smoking laws and there would always be blue lights, and I don't know what else. But this place was just a bar—no smoke or anything. It was very dark. Slow business, the bartender had time to lean. There was a decent band playing called the Golden Jones Trio. Golden Jones was apparently the sax man out front, but I was there for the bassist who was of course Joe Hayes, the almost-famous ex-husband of the late Louise Schaffer. He sounded good, not that I knew a toad's lick about jazz.

After his set, Hayes and I got to talking over cocktails at the bar. There was some perfunctory chit-chat and then we got down to business and Joe Hayes told me how Carter, the "little vampire," was not his kid. He was Schaffer's kid from her first husband.

Hayes said, "Louise and I were only married for a couple of months. It was just one of those stupid things. What the hell is this anyway? Why are you asking me all these questions?"

I was thinking I was some kind of real dumb-dumb. I just took what Rita the rent-a-cop had said as truth and ran with it. Then I found Joe Hayes's website which listed all of his show dates and I showed up at his earliest appearance.

He wanted to know why I was asking about Louise.

"You haven't heard?" I asked him.

"Heard what?" He wanted to know.

I told him.

Murdered, stabbed to death, the whole deal. I broke the news gently, but he still drained his glass and hailed the bartender for another drink. He was on his phone now, thumbing through news stories.

He said, "Shit. Aw. Lou."

I told him I was sorry.

He said, "I mean things were messed up between us. Hadn't talked to her for a few years, but ... Aw. I still loved her. I mean, I wasn't in ... well whatever. I loved her. Aw."

And so, the day just kept getting crappier.

I felt bad leaving the guy there after I'd dumped that news on him. I wasn't ruling him out as a suspect just yet, but I believed him for some reason. When I told him about the murder, it seemed like the only person he was worried about was Louise Schaffer. I saw the hope in his eyes when he pulled his phone, the hope that what I was saying was some mistake. Then I saw the hope being snatched away.

I left him there staring into his drink with his phone facedown on the bar. The late show band had started their set, a beach-tanned torcher in a blue dress accompanied by piano.

My car was parked a couple of blocks away, but it was a hot night and I didn't mind the walk. Outside the music faded as I walked away under the chorus drone of air conditioners in every window of the nearby apartment buildings. There was an old boxy sedan parked at the curb that looked familiar but I couldn't place it. As I walked past, the sedan's lights flicked on and it eased away from the curb. It rolled slowly, keeping pace with me for a few yards and then sped off. The windows were tinted black. I couldn't see anyone inside. I kept my whip bat in my hand until I was in my own car.

I calmed myself with the old "it's probably nothing" and drove home.

The next afternoon I was talking to Ray Gage's lawyer. She was a brick wall of a woman, but seemed sharp enough. Her office was a shared cubicle in the public defender's office in the county court building.

She was saying, "Of course my client didn't kill anybody. Why would he want to kill her? He was planning to 'ride that gravy train right into a new yacht.' Those are Mr. Gage's exact words."

I said, "Oh, I definitely believe that, but they heard her scream right after he boarded the boat. If he's innocent, he must have stumbled onto the real killer?"

"We've already told the police," she said. "That scream was from the little boy, Carter. My client walked into the boat's cabin with the boy and found Ms. Schaffer's body. It was a bloody mess of a scene. The kid flipped out as you can imagine. Now that is all I'm able to share about the case at this time, Ms. Belle."

So it was the kid screaming and not a woman at all.

"Poor kid," I said.

"Oh yes," she said. "Awful."

I told her, "Yeah, he's absolutely awful, but he didn't deserve to see his mom all stabbed that way."

She gave me a curious look laced with mild disgust.

I said, "Listen. Don't worry. I'm going to get to the bottom of all this."

Gage's lawyer told me she'd rather I didn't get involved. She knew all about me already. My help wouldn't be necessary. I told her I owed Gage for breaking his window. I had to help.

"Well," the lawyer shrugged. "That's logical."

"I can be very logical," I said.

She wanted to know what I planned on doing. I told her I was going to find Schaffer's first ex-husband and squeeze a confession out of him.

"Ah," she said. "I should've guessed. Good luck with that. By the way, what makes you think Jonathan O'Keefe is involved?"

"It's always the husband," I told her.

She nodded. Then she asked if that would be all and I took the hint. I was in the building's parking lot again heading home when I spotted the creepy sedan again.

I officially had a stalker.

I was back in my apartment talking to my dad on the phone and loading up my BB gun.

He was saying something along the lines of, "You sound like you're getting into another one of your things, Poopernickle. Remember how you get?"

How I get? I told him he was making me sound like some psycho.

He said. "I'm just worried about you, kid."

I promised him I'd be careful and hung up the phone. Dad, such a worry wart.

I hadn't even told him my plans for confronting Schaffer's first ex, Jon O'Keefe. O'Keefe was some big tech guy too, but even with his own success, he'd been marrying up with Louise Schaffer. I was nervous to confront him, but the plan was coming together in my mind.

I finished loading up my BB gun and then I went looking for my black pleather pants. I had to have a drink to calm my nerves. And it really was just for nerves, but one drink led to another and I woke up the next morning with bells ringing in my head and acid burning a hole in my stomach. I'd stripped my pleather pants off at some point in the night and they were still on my feet, inside out and stretched away from me on the bed like some rumpled shadow.

I had to get breakfast. I put on sweatpants, sneakers, shades and a big hat and walked to the corner Quickie shop. Ice cream. Coffee. Beer. Flamin' Hot Corn-chies. Breakfast sandwich. The usual.

Outside, the creepy car was there again, parked up ahead. I was in a bad mood, and I'd never responded nicely to intimidation in the first place, so I charged right at the car, running and screaming, arms full of groceries. Whoever was in there saw me and they sped away. I hurled a beer bottle at the car and it blasted across the back windshield. The driver panicked or something and drove up onto the sidewalk and into a no parking sign. The mangled signpost peeled off the car's front quarter panel like a sardine can and the car was gone in a cloud of blue tire smoke.

I was back on my dad's boat. We were in the galley and he was making omelets and smoothies. I had been telling him about what I'd been up to, including the creepy car that was stalking me. He was saying how now he knew I was "losing my head" and "getting into something" again.

I asked, "Do you really think O'Keefe or someone would have me stalked?"

He said he did, because why wouldn't they?

Dad goes, "These people have money to burn. If they feel threatened? Think about it. What would you do?"

Before I left, Dad made me promise to drop the whole thing and let the police handle it.

I'd been breaking promises to my dad as long as I could remember. He never broke one, none that mattered anyway. Someday I was going to have to make up for that.

The plan was simple. I was going to wait outside Jonathan O'Keefe's house and follow him. Watch him for a while. Track his movements. Maybe get some valuable intel. Wait for him to slip up. There were pictures of him online at some of these big tech conventions, always with the earpiece and grey hoodie. Plastic smile. Spray tan. Plugs. Just looking at his face I was pretty sure this was definitely my guy.

I had my gear. I had my little BB gun that most people would mistake for a real gun. I had my whip bat. I had some snacks, a bottle of gin and something to smoke. I was totally ready for a stakeout. I missed my brass knuckles. The Whip bat was cool and all, but it didn't charge me up the way the knucks did.

I hit my first speedbump when I came to the security roadblock at the gated cul-de-sac where O'Keefe lived in the hills. I tried telling them I was a rideshare driver there to pick up one of the residents, but the rent-a-cops weren't having it. They were on to me before I even rolled down my window. I wasn't used to security guards who cared. They told me to get lost before they called the police.

I was stumped. If it hadn't been purely for dumb luck, the whole investigation would come to a screeching halt right then.

I pulled over onto the shoulder just downhill from O'Keefe's cul-de-sac. The road was only-just wide enough for two cars, plus the narrow shoulder parking on one side. I was near a hairpin turn, parked and wondering what to do next when a car popped into my rearview. The grey sedan missing the front quarter panel.

I moved to follow it, brought my car to life and threw it in gear, but a little dew-drop of a sports car came behind the sedan, its mirror an inch from mine, and bingo—I recognized him from online photos. Jonathan O'Keefe in his little silver convertible. I fell in behind and the three of us snaked down the mountain until we came to a fork in the road. The sedan went off to the left. I stuck with O'Keefe. I didn't care about his hired goons anymore.

Technically my car was a sports car, about forty years ago, a little speed-back Japanese five-speed I named Buster. He was in good shape for his age and we both enjoyed pushing our limits through the turns. O'Keefe was flying down the mountain, taking the curves like a go-cart. I did my best to stay back without losing him or raising his suspicion. We were zipping along, his taillights always dipping in and out of sight. Then there was a red light at the bottom of the hill. Here the road straightened and went to two lanes in both directions. I brazenly pulled alongside O'Keefe and made a point of keeping my eyes forward. The light turned green and I let O'Keefe speed ahead. There was a red at the next intersection and I pulled up next to him again. We did that dance for a few blocks.

Then I figured he just went to work because I followed him to an office building where he parked and didn't leave for about six hours. The office building was poised near the edge of a creek-fed lagoon with views of the Pacific Ocean.

I got so bored. I wished Ray Gage was with me. He was the best on a stakeout.

I got on my phone and found out exactly where O'Keefe worked inside the building. The business had some techy sounding name like Gen-something or Something-gen. I walked right in the main building entrance, rode the elevator and then walked right in through the front door of O'Keefe's firm. There was an empty reception desk and open doors from the office lobby into a bullpen of cubicles. All of the cubicles were empty.

Was it Saturday?

There was a low and constant hum in the walls, the building breathing. I heard scattered clicks and whirs. I heard voices or at least one voice coming from the corner of the suite.

I tip-toed toward the sound down a stretch of six cubicles. My heart was pounding. I was ready to turn tail and bail on the whole thing, but I pushed ahead. I was right outside the corner office. It was all windows. I could see O'Keefe in there. He looked distraught, all red and puffy. He was mumbling something, then he threw a cocktail glass at the far wall and it exploded.

O'Keefe shouted, "I didn't have any choice." He must have been shouting at himself.

I ducked into a nearby cubicle so he wouldn't see me and now I could hear him mumbling to himself again. I couldn't hear super clearly but he was saying something like, "What have you done?" and then, "You killed her, that's what."

I was thinking, holy crap. The guy was talking to himself and confessing everything.

There was a split second when I thought about my dad saying "remember how you get," but then my brain started racing and everything went foggy with adrenaline and the next thing I knew I was charging into O'Keefe's office, screaming.

I said, "Citizen's arrest. You're busted."

I had my BB gun out. O'Keefe had a pistol. It was pointed right at me.

He screamed, "Ah. Whoa. Hey, who're you?"

I might have said, "Um."

O'Keefe recovered himself quickly. Then he demanded to know who I was and why I was charging into his office. He said he almost shot me. He pointed his gun at me a told me to put down the toy weapon.

"BB gun didn't fool you for a second, eh?" I said.

"Nope," he said. "Who are you?"

I said, "You're Louise Schaffer's ex aren't you."

He said, "Great another weirdo. I'm calling security."

"Aren't you?" I said.

He goes, "Aren't I what?

I asked him, wasn't he the ex-husband of Louise Schaffer.

He said he was.

Jon O'Keefe seemed to think it was funny that I thought he was the killer and that I could just come up here and arrest him. He locked his gun away inside a desk drawer and goes, "Why don't you put that thing away and I'll make us a drink. You look like you need one. God knows I do."

I holstered my BB gun. O'Keefe walked to a minibar in the corner and poured some stiff drinks. I didn't like his mockingly unthreatened manner. The guy was beyond arrogant but his whiskey was fine, went down easy and burned good, so I obliged his asshole-ish demeanor. He started talking but I stopped him and asked for another drink. He obliged. I took my time with the second.

He sat behind his desk and asked why I thought he would bother to kill his ex-wife.

"Love and money," I shrugged.

He nodded and said, "Of course." Then he took it upon himself to explain how those were the core motives for every homicide.

"You see," he said. "Love and money are an extended form of mating and food consumption. It's survival."

"Got any more of that whiskey," I said.

"Killing a member of the same species for the sake of one's own survival. It's a natural thing. The oldest motive there is."

He seemed like he was launching into a whole thing so I got up and poured myself a drink. I didn't like the way this guy was toying with me.

He said, "You're aware the police already have their man? They arrested someone for the crime two days ago."

"Yeah, Ray Gage."

"Yes, I believe that was it. Do you know him?

I drank more whiskey.

O'Keefe said, "Uh-huh. You did know him. I see. So you're here looking for some evil villain, looking for some way to prove I killed my wife. Well you're barking up the wrong tree." He goes, "Do you know the kind of lawyers I have? You never stood a chance. Really there's no point in coming up here and staging this—whatever this whole thing was."

He got up to mix himself another drink. He was explaining how coming up there with that "toy gun" and threatening him was a big mistake. He told me again how lucky I was, that he could have shot me and would have been well within his rights under self-defense.

"Who would blame me?" O'Keefe said.

I took the hint. This was him threatening me. Big mistake.

He was at the minibar with his back to me. I whipped out my bat and swung it right at the back of his skull. He must of heard me coming because he turned just in time and fell out of the way. I was off balance and he managed to grab the bat with both hands and wrenched it out of my hands.

I could tell he wasn't used to fighting. His wrenching made him square off and left him wide open. I pounced on him.

I jabbed left to his jaw, slammed a right into the other side of his jaw and kneed him in the groin. A fast combo like a rim shot. Ja-jaw nuts. Ba-dum tiss.

I'd put everything I had into it and O'Keefe folded over and vomited up all his fancy whisky.

Boxing these techy types was fun. Made me feel tough. I felt fantastic.

I got my whip bat back and told O'Keefe to stand up. He said he couldn't. He was making a big fuss, crying and spitting. I made myself another drink and had a smoke while I waited for him to suck-it-up. There was a moment where he made a pathetic lunge for the drawer that held the gun and I blasted his forearm to bits with the bat. He cried out and called me some horrible name.

I said, "Just be nice and do what I say or I'll keep hitting you."

"Do you know what kind of lawyers I have?" He said.

I said, "yeah, yeah," and poked his tummy with the baton. Poked him good.

He huffed and puffed for a second. I told him I was taking him to the police and to start walking.

He said, "The police? You actually believe what you're saying, eh? OK, yes police, actually. That's actually great. Yes, let's go to the police."

I walked him back through the office, past the cubicles, through the open reception room. I pushed the elevator call button and we stood there waiting.

O'Keefe wouldn't shut up. He was saying something about why would he kill Louise? He wasn't in love with her. Their divorce was finalized years before. He wasn't inheriting any money from her.

He said, "I have no reason to kill her."

The elevator door dinged open and I shoved him inside.

"Go to hell, man. You're going to prison," I told him.

"OK," he said. "One of us is going to jail. It might not be for murder, but one of us is definitely going to jail today."

"Whatever," I told him. "I heard you confessing, OK? You were all remorseful and saying how you had no choice, and what have you done and how you killed her. Didn't you actually say you killed her?"

"Yes, well," he said. "I wasn't a good husband to her. Quite a bad one actually. I drove her away. I drove her into the arms of men like that mad man who murdered her. I was a lousy spouse and it wound up getting her killed. I have regrets if that's OK with you."

The elevator doors opened onto the building lobby. I still didn't think Ray Gage was the murderer, but now I was starting to have doubts about O'Keefe too. And I realized that I didn't really know anything at all if I really thought about it. Also, if this guy didn't do it, I might actually go to prison for assault or kidnapping.

I marched him out to the parking lot. The boxy old sedan with the missing quarter panel was waiting for us.

I said, "Alright O'Keefe, call off your goons or I'll blister your face with BBs."

"Goons?" he said. "I have no idea what you're talking about, you moron."

"Come on," I told him. "Your henchman. In the car."

"Just when I think you couldn't get any more stupid," O'Keefe said. "I don't have any henchman."

"Who's in the car then?" I asked.

"How should I know?"

Then Thomas Dooley got out of the grey sedan. He looked excited and angry. He had a gun in his hand.

Dooley said, "Surprised to see me?" and raised his gun and aimed.

I pulled my BB gun and used O'Keefe as a human shield. I aimed the gun at Dooley. He aimed at us.

He said, "Put the BB gun down."

How did everyone know it was a BB gun?

I said, "No. You put your gun down."

Dooley said, "Screw you, bitch."

I was so tired of that word. I shot Dooley in the ear. It bled immediately.

Dooley squealed and squeezed his trigger. There was a ka-chunk from the gun and a thwack in O'Keefe's shoulder. I staggered. There was a dart with an orange poof sticking out of O'Keefe's arm. Dooley had tranquilized him.

Dooley was struggling to reload his tranq gun. He was saying how he bet I never saw him coming and bragged that it had been "him all along."

He was still monkeying with the gun when I smashed it out of his hand with the baton. I smashed hard a second time and his hand was mangled with a couple fingers bent wrong.

O'Keefe was going, "What was in that dart? What was in that dart?" But he trailed off and went to sleep.

Dooley was quivering on the ground clutching his broken hand.

I kicked the dart gun away and pointed my air pistol at Dooley and said, "So wait? You killed the wife?"

Dooley said, "Huh?"

"You said it was you all along," I told him. "You killed Louise Schaffer? Why? Some kind of complex revenge scheme on Gage?"

"What?" Dooley said. "Why would I have anything to do with that? Do you even listen to yourself?"

"Yeah. You're right," I said. "I know it sounds stupid. But why were you following me around?"

He shrugged, "I guess I got obsessed. You owe me for my medical bills. You smashed my face. And now my car."

His voice caught when he mentioned his mangled car and I think he teared up. Knowing Thomas Dooley, the car had probably been from some famous movie or TV scene. Some collector's item.

I asked him what he had been planning to do to me with that tranquilizer gun.

He told me he didn't have anything planned. He figured he would eventually catch me doing something dumb or illegal, then blackmail the money out of me for his medical bills.

"The gun was a prop," he said. "It didn't even work."

I was getting distracted.

I stopped Dooley talking and said, "OK, whatever. So who killed Louise Schaffer?"

Dooley said, "How should I know? The husband."

I said, "Huh?"

Dooley rolled his eyes and told me, "It's always the husband."

I said, "You mean this guy?"

He said, "If that's the husband, then yeah. He probably killed that lady."

I said, "So I was right? Awesome. High five?"

I held up my five, but Dooley just held his broken hand gave me the stank eye.

I guess someone had seen all of our gun-play and what-not, and they must have called the police because the next thing I knew I was being tackled by a bunch of cops.

The police arrested all three of us, Dooley, O'Keefe and me. After a night in jail and no sleep or booze I felt like crap. They released me without pressing charges. O'Keefe didn't want to press charges against me or Dooley and we both walked away unscathed, legally speaking. I guess O'Keefe had bigger problems. Apparently he confessed immediately. Caved like an eggshell and I had to wonder if his confessing had anything to do with whatever was in the dart. The district attorney filed charges on him within twenty-four hours.

I saw Dooley at Steve's Rinky Dink the next day. His hand was in a cast. There was a tense moment but he and I buried the hatchet over coffee. He said it was cool of me not to sell him out to the cops. I said "likewise" and we parted ways.

The story was everywhere in the news. Apparently, O'Keefe's own wealth was majorly exaggerated and he was on the edge of financial ruin. It turned out that there would have been some serious funds transferred into his account following the death of his ex-wife. He would've needed money to raise Carter alone. He probably still had a life insurance policy on Schaffer too. Framing Ray Gage was would have just been icing on the cake for Jon O'Keefe.

Love and money. Just like I figured.

A few days later I saw Ray Gage at the Seven Seas Saloon. He looked like a man who had just spent a few days in jail. He wore the same outfit he always wore. Blue jeans. Black T-shirt. Deck shoes. He had a black eye and his face looked hard boned and drained, underfed and shifty eyed.

"Gage," I said. "You made it."

He said yeah he made it. I asked him when he got out. He said only the day before, but he'd been hiding from news reporters.

"Your old man said I might find you here," Gage said. "I've got something for you."

He handed me a little white box with a red bow on it. It was heavy.

He said, "Just a token of gratitude for busting me out of the big house."

I opened the box and inside on a cushion of white batting was a beautiful set of brass knuckles with a dark gunmetal finish. I slipped them on and the cool metal sent a charge through my whole body. I felt amazing.

I said, "Gage, you shouldn't have."

As I was shadow boxing and testing the weight of my new knucks, Gage said, "Yes. I'm just realizing I probably really should not have."

I asked him if he knew what would happen to Carter.

He said, "Rich grandparents."

I nodded and we both laughed for some reason. Then he grabbed me into a chaste hug. It felt weird. We hadn't been hugging friends before.

He said, "You saved my life."

I said something like, "Er. Shut up, ya dork."

He still had me in a hug.

Gage said, "You don't understand. These people, powerful people like Louise's family, they can just take everything away from a guy like me anytime they want, just like that. I was on the hook, Daisy. I didn't think I was ever going to get off again. You saved my life. I think you're the best friend I've ever had. I freaking love you, Daisy."

I wrapped my arms around him and squeezed back.

I said, "Happy to help, Ray."

Then our drinks came.

UNDER WATER

Josh Pachter

"Uncle Frank," the eighteen of us called him, all the way through high school and for years thereafter.

Not to his face, of course. The only time we actually *met* our benefactor, after they'd bussed the group of us down to New York City for a "getting to know you" lunch in his midtown office, he was either "Mr. Robertson" or "sir." If he'd been wearing a ring and had held it out to us, I think most of us would have kissed it.

I know I would have.

We were a dozen and a half brainy teenagers, plucked out of public junior high schools around the country by the Robertson Scholars program and gifted with an education none of our parents could conceivably have afforded without Uncle Frank's generous support: four years—all expenses paid, including tuition, room and board, airfare home for holidays and summers and even a modest monthly allowance—at the elite Bellman Patterson Hall in Durham, Connecticut. Bellman Patterson, cobbled together in 1924 from the all-boys Bellman School and the all-girls Patterson Hall, was one of the two or three best private prep schools in the country. Off the top of my head, I can name eleven Nobel laureates and six Oscar-winning actors and actresses who were Bell Patt grads—as were seven senators, two vice presidents, and four presidential offspring.

And, thanks to Frank Robertson's benevolence, eighteen incoming freshman a year receive the benefit of a Bellman Patterson education, free of charge. I was one of the lucky members of the Robertson Scholars Class of 2004, as was Charlie Constantine, who I married in 2010, six years after graduation.

I grew up an only child in Parma Heights, Ohio, a blue-collar suburb of Cleveland. My parents—Mom a special-ed teacher at Parma Park Elementary, Dad a second-shift VPI operator at Swiger Coil—divorced when I was seven, and I shuttled back and forth between them until lucking into my Robertson scholarship. In contrast, Charlie spent his childhood in a classic nuclear family in Waterloo, Iowa, his folks happily married, with two older sisters to look out for him and a younger brother who worshipped him.

Which made it ironic, I guess, that I was the one who thrived in the Bellman environment, while Charlie couldn't handle being ignored by the rich kids and flunked out midway through our freshman year. We didn't know each other well in Durham—we Robertsons tended to hang out together, since we were pond scum compared to the scions of the wealthy who surrounded us and looked down their nose jobs at us, but Charlie and I just never clicked. He was into old movies and smoking pot—not necessarily in that order—and I was an ambitious bookworm, determined that, even though my clothes were shabbier than my classmates', my grades would speak for me and I would someday be successful enough to travel in their hoity-toity circles on my own merits, not just thanks to Uncle Frank's charity.

After Charlie left Durham and his parents stuck him in a military school back home, the rest of us never really talked about him, and no one stayed in touch with him. We were surprised when he showed up unannounced at our five-year class reunion in 2009, and stunned to see that he had apparently managed to straighten himself out—*despite* Woodward Academy, he told us, not *because* of it—and had recently graduated from the U of Iowa with a BA in English and Creative Writing and was working on a novel.

He and I connected at the reunion, squirreled ourselves off in a corner and talked about movies and books for hours—and, a year later, as I told you, we got married.

I had a terminal M.A. in European Literature from UConn, a decent job teaching world lit at Quinnipiac, and a modest one-bedroom apartment in New Haven, a four-minute walk from Frank Pepe's, home of the best clams-and-garlic white pizza you ever ate, but I wasn't planning on being a Bobcat forever. I was building my resume, aiming for an eventual Ph.D. and a tenured position at an R1—with all the prestige and financial security that would be a part of that package.

My apartment was cozy, and I liked it, but there was no way it was big enough for the two of us, let alone the family we hoped to start once Charlie finished his book and started bringing in a second income.

The real-estate bubble had recently burst, and we got a great deal on a gorgeous four-bedroom place in West Haven, three blocks from the beach. Charlie was resistant at first (though the owners were willing to let it go for a fraction of its value, money would still be tight on just my salary, and he thought we should wait until his novel was finished and he'd collected the big advance he knew it would earn), but one of the things I took away from my Bellman Patterson education was a hunger for the better—strike that: the *best*—things in life, and I managed to convince my new husband we could stand to be house-poor for a while, at least until he got his literary career in gear.

Everyone assured us the housing market was *bound* to improve, but as so often happens things got worse before they got better, and by the time we'd been married a year—much of which Charlie'd spent wrestling writer's block, making little progress on his book, and sipping gin-and-tonics on our living-room sofa—we were pretty deeply under water.

And then, ironically, on August 27, 2011—two weeks after our first anniversary—Hurricane Irene slammed into the Connecticut coast. Bridgeport and Groton were hit the hardest. We were lucky, compared to them, but we still wound up with a flooded basement it would cost eleven thousand dollars we didn't have to drain and repair. Our realtor had practically *begged* us to take out flood insurance, but we knew we'd barely be able to afford the mortgage payment as it was, and Charlie had finally given in to my insistence that a bigger house without the insurance would be preferable to a smaller one with it.

"Eleven thousand dollars," Charlie sighed.

We were in our kitchen on September first, hunched over steaming cups of Major Dickason's Blend in the little breakfast nook that had been one of the features that had sold us on the house in the first place. Irene had blown herself out somewhere over Eastern Canada, and the sun shone brightly in the afternoon sky.

I reached across the table and patted his hand.

"Where in the *world* are we going to find eleven thousand dollars?" he said.

I forced a smile. "Hey, we could be the only house on the block with an indoor swimming pool."

He stared at me blankly. Charlie never did have the world's greatest sense of humor, and we'd just survived a disaster that had done almost sixteen *billion* dollars' worth of damage, left thousands of people homeless across the Caribbean, knocked out power up and down the Atlantic Seaboard, and accounted for at least forty-nine deaths, so maybe this wasn't a great time to be kidding around.

"We could sell one of the cars," I suggested.

"For how much?" he asked gloomily. "A couple of grand, maybe, tops. That's nowhere near enough."

"Well, I've got reasonably decent credit. I'll take out a home-equity loan."

"And how are we supposed to pay it back, Connie? Besides, we haven't *got* any equity. We're under water as it is."

"Under water," I repeated, then switched to my Mork voice: "Humor, ah-ah."

My Mork voice usually cheered Charlie up when he was down, but not this time. "It's not funny, Con. We've got a serious problem here. Maybe you could drop your membership at your frou-frou gym and just join the Y like a normal person?"

I glanced down at my toned arms. I might have started my life in Parma Heights, but I was a Bellman Belle now, and there was no way I was going to wind up with what my mom used to call "bingo wings." In my adult life, working out was the closest thing I had to a religion.

"It's a *gym*," I said tightly. "There's nothing frou-frou about it. And all my friends go there. If you're going to sit on the couch and suck down the cocktails every night, I need *some* kind of a social life."

"You think those rich bitches are your *friends*? They don't care about people like us, Connie. They only pretend to like you because—"

Charlie was right: we *did* have a serious problem, here … just not the problem he thought we had.

So, okay, I thought, *it's time to get serious.*

"Maybe you could put the book aside for a while," I proposed, "and get an actual *job*."

He looked up from his coffee. "Doing what? My degree's in creative writing. I don't know how to *do* anything but write."

I licked my lips. "I love it that you write," I said, which had been the truth a year ago but had become less so over the last couple of months, even pre-Irene, as I'd gotten a good taste of what being house-poor actually *felt* like, "but your writing's not bringing in any *money*, Charlie, and right now we're in a jam. If you took a job in a bookstore, or a coffee shop, or whatever, you could make a couple hundred bucks a week, and that might cover the payments on a loan we could use to fix the damn basement."

A tear formed in the corner of his eye. "A couple hundred a week," he said, like I was offering an aspirin to a guy who'd just crawled out of a train wreck. "Jesus, I'd be worth more than that dead."

That caught my attention. "What do you mean?"

He cocked his head. "I never told you?"

"Told me what?"

He rubbed a palm across his face. "My folks were practical farm people. When we were kids, they took out a life-insurance policy on each of us. The day we turned twenty-one, they pulled us aside and filled us in—are you sure I never told you about this?"

I shook my head. "Nuh-uh, never."

He grimaced. "Well, since we're married, you're automatically my beneficiary.

When I croak, you collect a hundred K. Double that if I die in an accident."

"Double indemnity," I said. "Like the movie."

"Uh-huh."

"Can you cash in the policy? Maybe it's worth enough to—"

"Not an option. Remember what a screw-up I was at Bellman? When my parents saw what a loser I'd turned into, they did something to the policy so it can't be borrowed on or cashed in. You get the money when I die, but otherwise it's untouchable."

"Huh," I said.

"I need something stronger than coffee," Charlie frowned, getting up and heading for the living room. "You want a drink?"

"What's that?" I said, my mind elsewhere. "No, that's okay, you go ahead. I've got some thinking to do."

Three hours later, I eased myself out of the nook and found Charlie sprawled across the sofa, reeking of gin and tonic, dead to the world.

Dead to the world, I thought. *Talk about your irony.*

Did I mention I work out? Well, I do, four or five times a week—bench presses, biceps curls, triceps extensions—and I've got the upper-body strength to prove it.

I wrestled Charlie into our bedroom and managed to hoist him onto the bed. I stripped his clothes off him and let him lie there naked.

He'd really put on a lot of weight in the year we'd been married. I guess sitting around the house all day staring at a blank computer screen can do that to a guy. Not to mention the two or three G-and-Ts, night after night.

Exhausted, I went into the bathroom and drew a nice hot tub.

I like a hot bath, last thing before I go to bed, but tonight I had other plans.

I dragged Charlie into the bathroom and cracked the back of his skull against the porcelain, then dumped him into the water and held him down.

He struggled a little, but not for long, and then his body sagged and his mouth stopped bubbling.

Don't get me wrong: I love my husband.

Loved.

But two hundred thousand dollars will fix the basement and go a long way toward paying down the mortgage, and the money I'll save with Charlie gone will allow me to improve my wardrobe, maybe even buy some sessions with a personal trainer.

And a lovely home with no husband will take this Bellman Belle a lot further than a deadbeat husband with no home.

I'll bet Uncle Frank would agree with me.

You do, don't you?

A COZY ARRANGEMENT

A You-Solve-It By John H. Dromey

Not long after Julie Dupree inherited a big old rambling house and all the big problems that came with it, she decided the only affordable way to keep that particular roof over her head was to take in a couple of boarders. She went to her next-door neighbor Miss Hennessey for advice.

"There are no zoning restrictions," Miss Hennessey told her. "You should be careful, however, who you invite into your home. Some people behave worse than animals."

Sound advice, Julie concluded. She wanted to keep the wolf away from her door, but not by inviting a wolf in sheep's clothing to come inside.

With that in mind, the two women Julie selected were polar opposites. It was unlikely the pair of them would become bosom buddies and gang up on their landlady. If there were any minor disagreements, Julie felt confident she could act as an impartial referee to keep her lodgers from trying to kill each other. She was dead wrong.

The two tenants despised each other at first sight. One was abrasive, one was diffident.

Florence Porter, a fiercely independent health-food fanatic, abstained from alcohol, caffeine, nicotine, and fun foods in general. She prepared her own meals and knew a bland substitute for practically any tasty treat imaginable. Currently between jobs, her most recent employment had been as a caregiver for a diabetic shut-in. Flo filled her idle hours with knitting, needlework, and other craft projects. Despite her idiosyncrasies, in some ways she was an ideal tenant. At the start, she made few demands and paid her rent promptly.

Millicent Brubaker, in contrast, liked to read, relax, and be waited on hand and foot. Before suffering some financial setbacks, she'd been accustomed to staying in high-end hotels. With her very discriminating palate, she insisted her landlady place two pieces of rich, dark chocolate on her bedside table every night. Julie complied. She was determined to keep her quiet, well-behaved boarder content. The candies were always gone by morning.

Sparks flew whenever the two renters got together. Flo was a vociferous proponent of a Spartan lifestyle. For the most part, she stuck to her knitting. Give her an opening, though, and she'd commence to proselytize at the drop of a stitch. Millie, on the other hand, was soft-spoken and chose her words carefully while fiercely defending her own daily regimen. Even when apart, the two disparate women kept their simmering feud alive by complaining to anyone who'd listen. Julie got an earful several times a day.

Flo was a night owl. Millie was an early bird.

Just before her bedtime one evening, Millicent sought out Julie for a private conversation. In breathless hushed tones, she lodged a formal complaint against Florence. "That woman is a menace," Millie said. "A minute ago, when I passed her in the hallway, she jabbed me in the derrière with something—I assume it was a knitting needle. In any event, she drew blood. I may need a tetanus shot."

"I'm sorry, but there's nothing I can do about that right now," Julie said. "We'll talk again first thing in the morning before Flo gets up."

Millie went to bed. Julie cleaned up the kitchen. Flo watched a DVD on quilting.

When Millie did not show up for breakfast at her regular time the next morning, Julie went upstairs to investigate.

As soon as she discovered Millie's body, Julie called the police non-emergency number and then she called Miss Hennessey. The latter got there first, accompanied by a Yorkshire terrier.

Julie apologized for having roused her neighbor so early in the morning.

"You're not being a bother, dear. It was time for walkies anyway. If you'll mind Fluffy for me, I'll have a look around."

Julie failed to get a firm grip on the Yorkie's tether. The terrier went exploring, dragging its leash behind it. Julie did her best to keep up with the curious animal.

Unencumbered, Miss Hennessey took her time looking around the house. She began on the ground floor and finished in the attic. She looked everywhere except in the room where Florence was presumably still asleep.

Miss Hennessey found nothing out of the ordinary. Neither did the police— when they arrived—although the responding detective asked some routine questions anyway.

"She ate herself to death," Flo suggested, rubbing the sleep out of her eyes. "You saw the candy with a single bite out of one piece and the other still whole. Millie took one last guilty taste and had a heart attack. She was obviously dead long before I went to bed."

"There's no candy in her room now," Detective Rodriguez stated. "Did anyone else see it?"

"I did," Julie said.

"Do you know what happened to it?"

Julie blushed. "Miss Hennessey's dog ate it. The little rascal hopped on a chair, gobbled down the candy, and then scampered away."

Miss Hennessey blanched and cried out, "Poison!"

"You think someone injected a fast-acting poison into the candy?" the detective asked. "Who could have done that?"

Julie pointed at Flo.

"But I didn't!" Flo protested. She spun around and left the room with her head held high.

The Yorkie ran into the room. "Fluffy's okay," Miss Hennessey said with a sigh of relief.

"Does that mean the candy wasn't poisoned?" Julie asked.

"Not *only* that. It also means the candy wasn't even chocolate since Fluffy's allergic to the genuine article," Miss Hennessey said. "There has to be another explanation for what happened here last night. I have an inkling of an idea, based on what you told me about your boarders. I suspect Millie's death was the result of foul play."

Julie didn't know what to think. She was momentarily speechless.

Solution in next month's issue ...

SOLUTION TO OCTOBER'S YOU-SOLVE-IT

The Missing Train by Kate Fellowes

As a trained librarian, when Melissa browsed Suzanne's books, she automatically shelved them according to the rules of the library. While Suzanne put her books in alphabetical order, spelling out the numbers in the title—*the Four-Fifty from Paddington*—Melissa had moved the book to the beginning of the collection, since numbers are placed before letters in a library setting.

Emily trotted to the shelves, plucking the precious title from its new location before presenting it to a humbled Suzanne.

"What? What did I do?" Melissa asked as Emily and Deb laughed.

"What you do best, dear," Emily told her. "You organized."

SOLUTION TO OCTOBER'S YOU-SOLVE-IT

Lost In Time By Peter DiChellis

With the murderer in custody, the elated Bumbler queried the Great Detective. "My God, man. How did you solve it?"

"Elementary. The killer revealed himself with a readily observable error, while the remaining two suspects were eliminated by simple deduction."

"Simple deduction?" The Bumbler wailed. "The gardener's receipt was time-stamped 8:34, half an hour before the murder. And he drives a V-8 pick-up truck that could capably speed him to the victim's home."

"But all northbound traffic was obstructed by the Loose Chicken Blockage, preventing any chance the gardener could have driven from the south side at high speed."

"And how did you deduce the former co-worker used his cellphone from his own home, not the victim's home, despite his false statement about the time the call ended?"

"I simply reasoned he didn't beat someone to death while talking with his mother."

"And the husband's readily observable error?"

"Only the husband," the Great Detective continued, "would have wiped his bloody fingerprints from the murder weapon but not needed to wipe his prints elsewhere in the house."

"Because there's nothing suspicious about finding his fingerprints in his own home."

"Precisely. But he couldn't leave them in blood on the hammer."

"And the football-watching party he attended …"

"… was right next door. He easily sneaked away during a bathroom break. The telltale clue was not the time of the murder, but the discrepancy between the killer wiping fingerprints from the hammer yet leaving prints everywhere else."

And so, due to the Great Detective, the killer would now spend his time in prison.

Made in the USA
Middletown, DE
11 February 2022

60994130R00049